Lost in the Enchanted Forest

A Young Adult Fantasy

By
Sandi Jerome

Kira and Henry

Lost in the Enchanted Forest

A Young Adult Fantasy

By
Sandi Jerome

SmilingEagle Press Book

1st Edition

© 2025 by Sandi Jerome

Published by SmilingEagle
A Native American imprint of Little Studio Films Publishing
For information:
SmilingEagle Press
www.smilingeagle.com

ISBN: 978-1-7360348-9-7
Printed in the United States of America

Cover Design by: Nilesh Prabhu
author.nileshprabhu@gmail.com

Map and drawings by: Tulaasi Jerome
https://www.etsy.com/shop/RainbowJunkieINC

Dedication

This book is dedicated to my fearless women warriors; Chandra, Suby, Tulaasi and Vrinda who have made my life an adventure and my husband Keith who has taken the ride with me.

Kira and Henry
Lost in the Enchanted Forest

A Young Adult Fantasy

Sandi Jerome

Map of the Kingdom

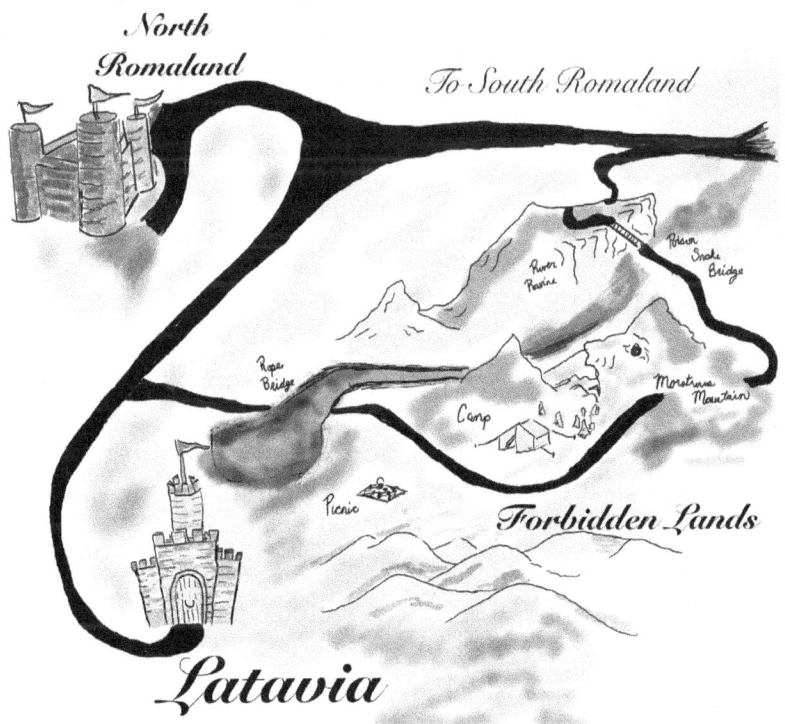

Prologue

Princess Kira had always trusted her instincts in battle, but nothing had prepared her for this. The ancient trees of the enchanted forest loomed above her, their branches swaying together like a living ceiling that blocked out most of the afternoon sun.

Every fiber of her raptor being screamed at her to take to the skies, and soar above the canopy where she could see all threats approaching. But the old laws of Latavia bound her wings inside her tunic as surely as chains – raptor were forbidden to fly from birth. If discovered, she would be exiled out of the kingdom, her kingdom, even a royal princess. As she rode her horse Julius with her sword ready at her side, something felt different about this place. The very air seemed to hum with an energy that made her skin prickle.

"The forest is thicker than I expected," she called to Henry, who rode beside her on his steed, Augusta. They had entered these legendary woods on what should have been a simple quest, but already Kira sensed they were no longer in control.

Kira pulled a red rope from her saddlebag, her expression determined. "Before there were map makers like your precious Nesta, people used this method to find their way back. "

Henry watched her tie the rope to a massive oak near what appeared to be a path and smiled. Yes, Princess Kira was his future ruler, but was there something more in that statement? Was his childhood friend, Kira jealous of the attention he was giving Nesta?

"You keep the red rope on your right when going somewhere, then collect it on your left coming back," Kira instructed. The moment Kira completed the binding, the ground began to rumble.

Kira's warrior instincts kicked in immediately. Her raptor blood surged, demanding she spread her wings, but instead she reached for her sword as the earth beneath Julius was already shifting and cracking. The wind whipped through the branches with supernatural force, and she fought to control her startled horse.

"Henry!" she shouted, but her voice was lost in the growing roar. Thick roots erupted from the forest floor like serpents, wrapping around her legs before she could react. These weren't ordinary roots – they moved with purpose, with intelligence. Kira struggled against them, her sword useless as more vines climbed higher, binding her arms. She was being plucked from her horse and the last thing she saw before darkness claimed her was Henry's shocked face as they were both dragged upward into the canopy, hundreds of feet above the ground.

When consciousness returned, Kira found herself hanging upside down, suspended by enchanted vines in a circle of enormous trees. But these weren't just trees – they had faces. Ancient, wise, and unmistakably alive.

"This one is waking up," said a voice that sounded like her mother. But that was impossible. Her mother was dead. Kira had killed her.

Kira's eyes snapped open fully, her training keeping her alert despite the disorientation. Three massive feminine faces studied her with expressions ranging from curiosity to outright hostility.

"Where are our children?" demanded the angriest of the three, leaning so close that Kira could smell earth and musty leaves on her breath.

Princess Kira had faced armies, the monstrous mountain, the poisoned snake bridge and even made friends with twin trolls, but nothing had prepared her for talking trees that held her prisoner in their branches. As she hung there, defenseless and at their mercy, she realized this quest had become something far more dangerous than anyone had imagined.

The enchanted forest had awakened, and it was very, very angry.

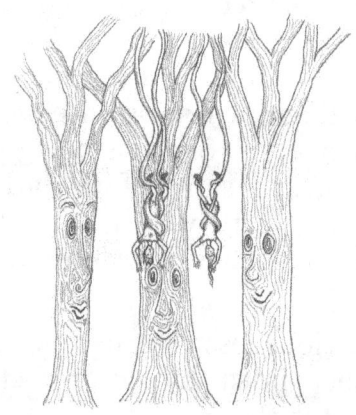

Sandi Jerome

Chapter 1 - Finding Kira

 The two trolls tracked the small boy. They stopped to sniff and look at his footprints. It has been hours since their last meal, and between them, they usually ate the equivalent of a baby deer by this time of the day. The sun was peeking out between the green rolling hills in the distance and soon it would be dawn. They were hungry and ugly, as you would expect of medieval trolls early in the morning. Their enormous noses enabled them to smell the boy, and he smelled delicious. Those smells fueled their frenzied hunt. "This way," Peek insisted as he pulled his twin towards a dark cave.

"He would never go there," his brother protested. "He's smart, and he wouldn't let himself get cornered like a helpless animal," his brother added.

Peek sniffed. He looked up and pointed at a thick tree. "He is close, up there, maybe?" Peek dragged his brother close to the tree. It was a difficult task because they shared a single oversized tunic. If one troll was terrifying, a pair of hideous twin trolls conjoined at the hip was a frightening sight. The pair starred up into the tree.

"I can't see anything," Peek said as he sniffed loudly again. His brother joined him in the sniffing. They raised their heads, puzzled. He turned to the right and sniffed and then to the left.

Peek lowered his head slightly and sniffed again. "He is not up there, but his scent is close," Peek said.

The boy giggled. He was standing right behind them. They tried to turn around in opposite directions. Unfortunately, neither their body nor their tunic allowed them to move. Finally, they both bent down and peered between their legs. Victory! They had found Henry and the juicy turkey legs tucked into his belt.

"Left," Peek ordered his brother. Then, with a coordinated effort, the pair spun around and lifted Henry into the air. Henry was a squire of about twelve but slight for his age. The twin trolls were three times his size. Each grabbed a juicy leg and dropped Henry to the ground.

"Ouch," Henry said as he stood up and dusted himself off. He glanced at the sun, shielding his eyes. "That was your best time ever." The trolls beamed with pride. They liked making Henry happy. Peek frowned while his brother, Aboo continued smiling.

"What is wrong? Aboo asked when he saw his brother also staring at the sun rising in the distance.

"Henry is going to be late. You know how the princess hates it when he is late," Peek said. Henry jumped on his horse and rode off before Aboo could answer.

There were three things that Henry was good at; finding things, training horses, and sword fighting. He was not good at being on time. Kira complained that it was because he didn't respect her. Yes, she was the young and fearless teen Princess of Latavia who would ascend to the throne someday, but to Henry, she was the spoiled and entitled playmate that he had grown up with.

Kira lived in the castle and he lived in the stables. She was a princess and he was a squire, a position so low it wasn't even listed on the hierarchy of the castle. First there was the monarchy, then the Lords. After that were the knights, then the peasants/serfs. A squire didn't exist since they were considered the property of a knight; no different than a sword or a shield. At the end of the great quest, Kira had knighted him, but later the Knight's council had invalided his knighthood. "Sir Henry," they laughed. You're a squire.

But if a squire were to prove he was worthy, then his knight might start training the squire to be a real knight someday. The only problem for Henry was that he grew up as a squire with no knight. Instead of being the slave of a knight, he was Kira's slave. He had proven himself worthy last year when Kira's step brother had been kidnapped and she was blamed, but when Kira "knighted" him, it was quickly reversed when they got back to the castle due to his age.

At thirteen, Henry too young to be a knight according to the great book. He had gone back to being a knight-less squire and even the other squires treated him like a serf. But when he turned thirteen, things would change. There was only one problem; and it was a problem that nobody else had.

This morning at five bells, he woke up hungry as usual. After he quickly did his chores, racing to get done before six bells, the smell from the castle ovens where they had already started preparing the feast was overwhelming this morning. He knew it was only a matter of time before his troll friends, Peek and Aboo would be caught stealing food, so Henry snuck in and grabbed two turkey legs and convinced his pals that a game of "finding Henry " would be more fun that trying to sneak into the castle kitchen.

His horse, Augusta, was even better than Henry at finding things. With his long nose, he could smell over a thousand chains away. Kira required that each morning before breakfast that Henry find her and then duel with her until he let her win. For him, it was more like the childish game of "hide and seek" than training to be a knight.

♠

Princess Kira glared at the rising sun between the tree branches. He was late again, Kira thought. She stood on a peaceful grassy knoll high above the castle. The leaves were starting to turn blood red.

It will soon be winter, and winter means war, she thought. Her face was stone cold, and her sword held high. Kira prepared for battle. She warmed up with some practice lunges and masterful footwork.

Her horse fed nearby on the green grass under the large shade tree as Henry rode up next to it and quickly jumped off and ran towards her. "I know, I know," Henry said as Kira pointed her sword at his sword. But, unfortunately, it was still in the sheath. So he struggled to get it out and run at the same time.

"The enemy himself provides the opportunity of defeating the enemy. You are not ready to fight," she said. She lunged toward him, and the swordplay began. Although Henry was slight and young like a squire, he had the confidence and skills of a knight. After a few minutes, it appeared that he could easily take the princess but eased up when things got too close.

"You better be on time tomorrow for your party," Kira said.

"I hate my birthday," Henry replied.

"Our birthday, it is my birthday too." Kira sensed Henry was distracted and went in for the kill. He backed up and tripped, falling to the ground. With a couple of swift moves, she held the sword to his chest.

"Surrender!"

"I give up. You win, again," Henry said as he pushed her sword aside and got up. Then, after dusting himself off, he sat down on a large rock and wiped the sweat from his forehead. Next, he unbuckled his sword belt and dropped it to the ground.

Kira sat down next to him, "I know you're worried."

"I'm not worried. It is just...."

She patted him kindly on the shoulder. It was awkward for her. "Getting your first quest, your official knight's tunic, and your own troop...it is a lot for a young boy."

Henry stood up, angry. "Young boy?"

Kira realized her error. "Sure, you're turning thirteen, and I might have made you knight, but until our party tomorrow."

"Don't you get it?" Henry jumped up and faced her, his face as red as the leaves falling around him to the ground. "Nobody knows my real birthday. When your people killed my parents and took me as a slave, they didn't ask first, "when is the little boy's birthday so we can celebrate it after you're dead?"

He stormed toward the horses. He turned around to see if Kira was following. Nope, Kira always stood her ground, never giving up an inch of territory. Kira crossed her arms.

"It is your birthday, not mine," Henry added. Henry got on his horse, Augusta. He took one more look back at Kira and then took off. Kira walked slowly to her horse.

"You may be excused, Sir Henry."

♠

The horse stable was the one place where Henry felt at home. He was good with horses, and they didn't treat him like a Romalander slave. Henry fed his horse, Augusta, while brushing his horse's coat.

As Henry stroked him, he whispered in the horse's ear. Then, finally, Henry looked longingly out the window to the east.

"Yes, that is Romaland, where I was born."

Augusta nodded and neighed.

"I don't know, maybe about two or three years old. I can't remember."

Augusta stamped his foot three times.

"Okay, probably when I was three. When the knights brought me to the King, it was Kira's birthday. So, while they decided what to do with me, I started playing with Kira and opening her presents. So, they sang Happy Birthday Kira and Henry."

The stable door creaked open, and Mark and James stumbled in, clearly having been drinking. They were singing loudly and off-key, "Happy birthday, dear Henry, happy birthday to you!" Their voices were mocking, and they swayed as they approached Henry's stall.

"Well, well, if it isn't the birthday boy," Mark slurred, leaning against Augusta's stall. "Thirteen years old tomorrow, little Romalander."

Henry stood up straight, his jaw tightening. "I will be a Latavian knight."

James laughed harshly. "Knight? You're nothing but a slave who got lucky. You should be grateful we don't send you back to Romaland where you belong."

"I earned my place here," Henry said, his voice steady despite his anger. "I saved Prince Alec and proved my loyalty to Latavia."

"Your loyalty?" Mark spat. "Once a Romalander, always a Romalander. You can't change your blood, boy."

Henry stepped forward, his fists clenched. "I've done more for this kingdom than either of you ever have. You were the ones who believed Peter's lies and thought Princess Kira was the kidnapper. You're the real traitors here."

"How dare you!" James shouted, pushing Henry hard in the chest.

Henry stumbled back but quickly regained his footing. He pushed James back even harder, sending the drunken knight into the hay. "I dare because it's the truth!"

Mark drew his sword halfway from its sheath. "I'll teach you to respect your betters, slave."

Henry's hand went to his own sword. "Try it. I'm not the frightened three-year-old you remember."

Before either could draw their weapons fully, Charles appeared in the stable doorway. His commanding presence filled the space, and both Mark and James immediately sobered.

"What's going on here?" Charles demanded, his voice carrying the authority of years of command.

Mark and James exchanged guilty looks. "Nothing, sir," Mark mumbled. "Just wishing the boy a happy birthday."

12

Charles studied the scene – Henry's defensive stance, the hay scattered from the scuffle, the tension in the air. "Is that so? Then perhaps you should return to your quarters and sleep off whatever you've been drinking."

James gave Henry one final shove, sending him tumbling back into the hay next to Augusta. "This isn't over, Romalander," he hissed.

As Mark and James stumbled out of the stable, Charles approached Henry, who was brushing hay from his tunic.

"Are you hurt?" Charles asked.

Henry shook his head. "No, sir. Just tired of being reminded where I came from."

Charles placed a firm hand on Henry's shoulder. "A wise man once told me that we're not defined by where we come from, but by the choices we make. You've made good choices, Henry. Don't let fools like them make you forget that," he said as he turned and left the stables.

Augusta dropped his head sadly as Henry dusted himself off. Henry lifted the horse's head and looked firmly into Augusta's eyes.

"Don't you ever tell her about this, or that I was complaining. It is just..." Henry looked to the east again. "...maybe someday, we'll go home and find someone who knows my family, and I'll know my real birthday."

♠

The following day Kira stretched and yawned loudly. Her lady-in-waiting, Alice, entered the room with a handful of clothes. "Happy thirteenth birthday, Princess."

"It is a great day!" Kira said as she jumped up and inspected the clothes. Her smile quickly turned into a frown. "I need to train the troops, not practice my dancing."

Alice smiled. Under the gowns were Kira's standard tunic and pants. Alice had been through this routine before. "Sorry, my lady. I thought because of the party tonight...."

"A wise ruler never lets his guard down. But, unfortunately, there has been unrest close to our borders. So maybe those Romalanders need a taste of my sword again."

Alice was trained by her mother to let Kira command the conversation while she continued to help Kira into her clothes.

"In North Romaland, King Stephen is having difficulty with those still loyal to King Alexander. In South Romaland, I heard that Owen, Dirk, and Bart are up to their old tricks." Kira broke away from Alice's fussing with her tunic and grabbed her sword. She started to fight an invisible opponent. "Let them try to kidnap me again, and I will run them through. I am no longer a little girl."

Alice nodded, agreeing with the princess, but she knew better. Last year, Queen Selina's brother, Peter, kidnapped Kira's stepbrother, Prince Alec. Peter thought the new prince was King Phillip's child and did not want the alliance between Latavia and Romaland that the joining of the two families would cause. Neither did Princess Kira.

Alice's mother had practically raised Princess Kira after Kira's mother had died when Kira was about five. The princess had fiercely trained her whole life to rule Latavia. Then King Phillip gave refuge to Queen Selina, the widow of King Alexander, during the Romaland civil wars. Their quick wedding was a surprise, and then Prince Alec was born. The Latavia law dictated that a male, Prince Alec, would become the next Latavia king instead of a female, Princess Kira.

Many suspected Kira as the culprit behind the kidnapping of little Prince Alec. So, Kira and Henry went on a quest into the forbidden lands to save Prince Alec. Together, they restored Kira's honor and her future path to the crown. She had knighted Henry for his bravery on the battlefield, but it was not official. "Our birthday party will change all that," Kira thought.

Kira finished her sword practice and put the sword into her sheath belt. "A wise ruler thinks of others before herself. It is Henry's birthday, and I must plan."

Alice smiled as the princess left her chambers, leaving a trail of nightclothes and partially eaten first breakfast. What Kira lacked in social skills and diplomacy, she made up with loyalty and fierceness.

The tunic maker's shop was small, but Grace, the owner, took pride in her establishment. She displayed rolls and rolls of fabric evenly by their hues. On the wall behind the counter was an attractive display of an array of coats of arms, all hanging neatly.

Kira walked quickly up and down the aisles, pointing at a roll of green fabric with her sword. It tumbled to the ground. Trailing behind her, Grace scurried quickly to grab it. "Excellent choice, Your Highness! This particular shade of green is from the lovely trees of...."

Kira held up her hand to silence her. She pointed to a gruesome coat of arms on the wall with her sword. It depicted a single knight with half a dozen fallen knights around him. Blood spurted up and dripped from the knight's sword.

"I am so sorry, Your Highness. I should have removed that. But, unfortunately, it is the ancient coat of the Bedlander clan; I don't think any of them are still alive -- I guess you can see why," Grace said.

Kira studied it closely. "It is perfect! The blood will stand out on that green."

Grace's face initially showed shock, but she recovered before Kira noticed and carefully nodded.

"Henry will love this. Have a dozen of these sewn on green tunics by noon and at the castle. But two of them must be very big and with an odd design. So, you will need to get a team of seamstresses here to get them done," Kira commanded.

"They are already busy at work this morning. We had a feeling the tunics would be green."

Kira handed Grace a scroll. "This is the size and design of the big ones. Then, wrap one of the dozen smaller ones. I want it to surprise Henry," Kira said as she looked at the scroll again.

"On second thought, wrap the big ones too," Kira added.

♠

The King's chancery was a commanding room consumed by a huge wooden and ornate desk. Behind it sat King Phillip, who was also a commanding man but with kind eyes for his daughter, Kira. "It is official," the king said as he signed a scroll and affixed his seal before handing it to Kira. "Henry is Sir Henry today."

Kira blows on the seal. "I had no idea that the law said that I must be thirteen when I knighted him after Alec was kidnapped. What a stupid rule."

"A wise ruler knows that there is a reason for these laws," her father said with his deep, yet gentle voice.

Kira rolled up the scroll and put it in her belt. "He deserved it years ago. If it was not for Henry, they would have killed Alec and framed me for it."

"Neither you nor Henry were old enough for that quest. If only your mother could see what a strong young lady you have become..." He went around the desk and put his arm around her. "..and a great warrior. You and Henry will command the next quest."

"A Quest? Where? What? I am dying to know!" Kira had transformed from the confident warrior into a little girl.

The king smiled slyly, "You will have to wait until the party tonight to find out. What color did you choose for Henry's new troop? The coat of arms?"

Kira turned around, but winked first at her father. "You will have to wait until the party to find out." The warrior had returned.

Chapter 2 - A Knight's Reward

The morning sun cast long shadows across the jousting field in Romaland as broken lances littered the ground like fallen soldiers. Owen wiped sweat from his brow as he inspected the knight's weapon, his weathered face showing concern.

"Your lance looks like it is made from the trees of West Latavia, but that cannot be," Owen said, running his fingers along the smooth wood.

The victorious knight removed his helmet, revealing the handsome face of Prince William, King Stephen's nephew. His dark hair caught the sunlight as he smiled with the confidence of one who had never known defeat. The gathered maidens sighed at the sight of him, while the men shifted uncomfortably.

"Treaties are meant to be broken," Prince William said, examining his own lance with satisfaction. "Why shouldn't we enjoy the fruits of the ancient lands of song and celebration?"

Owen's eyes darted nervously toward the western border. "Because we'd be shot on sight if we entered West Latavia."

Prince William laughed a sound both charming and dangerous. "The Latavians never go there anymore. They believe all the myths of it being an enchanted forest. They worry soldiers will never come back." The prince held up his lance, noting the many dents from previous jousts. Each mark told a story of victory, of opponents defeated by the strength of this mysterious wood. "Three purses of gold for you and your idiot friends to go into the forest and bring me back logs," he said, his voice carrying the easy authority of royalty.

Owen paused, looking over at his companions, Dirk and Bart, who stood nearby picking their teeth with splinters from the broken lances. They were rough men, scarred by years of doing the dangerous work that nobles preferred to avoid. "We need six bags of gold to risk our lives," Owen countered. "The Latavians surely remember our failed attempt to kidnap their princess and your cousin, Alec."

Prince William's expression darkened at the mention of the failed mission. "Yes, they thought Alec was Prince Phillip's son and future heir to Latavia. Stupid Latavians, they deserve to lose their kingdom and those enchanted lands too!"

Owen scratched his beard thoughtfully. "Even your father, King Stephen, didn't realize Alec was your uncle's child and the next heir to all of Romaland. If we had known, we would have killed that brat when we had him."

"Yes, Alec does pose a threat," Prince William admitted, his handsome face twisting with frustration. "But now that he and my Aunt Selina live in the protection of King Phillip of Latavia, I doubt if we'll ever have another chance. Our best future lies with conquering all of Latavia." He held up the lance again, feeling its perfect balance and strength. "This wood might be the key to making thousands of strong weapons quickly, but I need more to give to the blacksmith to find out."

Without ceremony, he tossed several heavy purses at Owen's feet. The coins clinked together with a sound that made all three men's eyes light up with greed. "Consider this a start of many riches that will come your way once you figure out how to easily get in and out of that forest," Prince William said, already turning away as if the matter was settled.

Owen bent to gather the gold, his mind already racing with plans. The enchanted forest had nearly killed them last time, with its talking trees and giant fireflies. But gold was gold, and Prince William's ambitions could make them all rich men.

As the prince walked away, Owen looked at his two companions. Dirk was already counting his share of the coins, while Bart stared longingly at the strong lance. "When do we leave?" Bart asked, his voice a mixture of excitement and fear.

"Soon," Owen replied, pocketing his gold. "But this time, we go prepared."

♠

Princess Kira's bed overflowed with green tunics, each one displaying the gory coat of arms that had become Henry's symbol. Alice, her faithful lady-in-waiting, helped her straighten out the new tunic, wincing slightly at the graphic design of blood and battle. "Wonderful, isn't it?" Kira said, holding up the tunic with obvious pride. "I thought I would wear it to honor Henry tonight."

A soft knock interrupted their conversation, and Alice rushed to open the door. Queen Selina entered gracefully, holding a beautiful gown of deep blue silk that seemed to shimmer in the morning light. "Happy birthday, Princess," Queen Selina said warmly, though her smile faltered slightly when she saw the garish green tunic.

Kira's face fell at the sight of both her stepmother and the elegant gown. The queen held out the dress hopefully. "I had this made to match your eyes," Queen Selina continued. "You will look stunning in this tonight."

Kira smoothed her green tunic defiantly. The queen tried to hide her shock at the violent imagery emblazoned across the front. "I am already dressed," Kira announced firmly. "I wear Henry's new colors to honor him. Do you like it?"

Queen Selina struggled to find the right words. "It is... colorful and graphic."

Kira pointed to a wrapped present on her bed, her voice growing more enthusiastic. "It is a present for Henry. I had a dozen of these made for him and his new troop."

The queen's eyebrows rose in concern. "But if you wear that, it won't be such a surprise for Henry's birthday?"

Kira paused, considering this wisdom. Then she slipped her old tunic over the ghastly green one, covering the bloody design. "Yes, the art of war is deception," she said with satisfaction. "Thank you for reminding me of that."

As Queen Selina watched her stepdaughter's preparations, she couldn't help but worry about Kira's single-minded focus on warfare and battle. But she also admired Kira's loyalty to Henry, even if she questioned Kira's motivation. Henry was a Romalander like herself and at times, she thought of him as another son.

♠

Queen Selina returned to her bedroom empty-handed, the rejected gown draped over her arm like a symbol of her failed efforts. King Phillip sat on the edge of their bed, looking up hopefully as she entered.

"She took it? She will wear her new gown tonight?" he asked, though her expression already gave him the answer.

The queen shook her head sadly. "I should have had you take it to her." She sat down beside him, the weight of her relationship with Kira pressing down on her shoulders. "She hasn't forgiven me."

King Phillip took her hand gently. "Give her time. It is hard for those without children to understand what someone would do to protect their child. You did it for Alec. She had no idea he wasn't my son. I should have told her."

"Any child would resent someone marrying their widowed father," Queen Selina said, her voice thick with emotion. "But to add betrayal to my crimes was too much for Kira to handle."

The king squeezed her hand reassuringly. "Give her more time, and then a little more. Kira needs that. I know she will forgive you for both someday. You were out of your mind after they kidnapped Alec."

He studied her face, seeing the pain that still haunted her eyes. "I was so distraught that I came to believe that Kira was responsible. She forgave me. She will forgive you like I did."

Queen Selina leaned against his shoulder, drawing comfort from his strength. "I never thought I'd be happy or love again after King Alexander was murdered by my own brother, Peter." She gave him a gentle kiss on the cheek, her voice soft with gratitude. "I love you more each day. You better get ready."

She picked up a small package from her dressing table, her expression becoming slightly amused. "And you need to brace yourself for this ghastly tunic she will be wearing."

King Phillip cocked his head; his curiosity was growing about this tunic. How bad could it be?

♠

Henry sat solemnly in the courtyard, watching the parade of carts pulling up to the great hall. They were loaded with food and decorations for the birthday party that he wasn't sure he wanted. The bustle of preparation seemed to mock his inner turmoil about his identity and place in the world.

Queen Selina spotted him from across the courtyard and approached with her young son, Prince Alec, who carried a small wrapped present in his chubby hands. The moment five-year-old Alec saw Henry, he broke into a run.

"Henry, Henry! I got you a horse!" Alec exclaimed, his childish excitement infectious.

The queen smiled as she caught up with her son, who had already begun unwrapping Henry's present without ceremony. "So much for the surprise."

Alec grabbed the golden horse statue from the wrappings and thrust it into Henry's hands. "I named him Little Gus after your own horse, Augusta."

Henry held the beautiful figurine, his eyes widening with recognition. "It is beautiful and somewhat familiar."

"Real gold," Alec said proudly. "We took one of the dozens of horses you carved for me and paid a nice man to cover it in real gold."

Henry's throat tightened with emotion as he realized the significance of the gift. Gold? He had never owned anything like this. He looked up at Queen Selina, who smiled knowingly. Recovering his composure, he reached into his tunic pocket and pulled out a wooden version of the same horse.

"I have a present for you, too," Henry said, offering it to the little prince.

"It's not my birthday," Alec pointed out, but he grabbed the wooden horse anyway. He immediately dropped to his hands and knees and began galloping the toy across the courtyard, making enthusiastic horse sounds.

Henry looked again at the golden horse, obviously deeply moved by the thoughtfulness of the gift. "It is too much."

Queen Selina sat beside him on the stone bench, placing a gentle hand on his shoulder. "I owe you so much more. You saved Alec from the Romalanders who wanted to kill him to protect King Stephen's throne."

"Our own people..." Henry said quietly, the pain still fresh in his voice.

The queen nodded sadly.

"I was taken from the North, a village called Cedarshire. Do you know anyone from there?" Henry said and the Queen smiled, obviously remembering her homeland.

Henry's heart leaped with hope, but Queen Selina shook her head regretfully. "That village was mostly destroyed a decade ago during the last war between Romaland and Latavia." She patted his shoulder sympathetically. "I'm sorry, Henry. But I hope you will think of King Phillip and Kira as your family now... and Latavia as your home."

She rose to collect Alec, but turned back to look at Henry one last time, then at her son playing happily with his wooden horse. "I have."

♠

Inside the great hall, servants worked frantically to prepare for the birthday celebration. Long tables groaned under the weight of fruits, desserts, and presents. But the strangest sight of all was in the corner, where the massive twin trolls, Peek and

Aboo, were carefully lifting the tunic-maker Grace so she could hang colorful streamers from the rafters.

Kira entered the hall and surveyed the bustling activity. When she spotted the trolls, she called out to them.

"Aboo, Peek!"

The pair turned around quickly, leaving Grace hanging precariously from the rafters. Her screams echoed through the hall as she dangled helplessly. Kira rolled her eyes and pointed upward.

"Careful with her!"

The trolls looked up, realized their mistake, and gently plucked Grace from the rafters, setting her down safely. Despite their fearsome appearance, their eyes showed only kindness and concern.

"Have you seen Henry?" Kira asked.

The twins shook their heads in unison. "Maybe he is in the stables feeding Gus?" Peek suggested hopefully.

Aboo nodded in agreement. "He likes to give Gus a carrot about this time of day."

Kira considered this, then smiled with an idea. "Go fetch him for me. I want to give him his birthday present early."

The trolls exchanged excited glances and hurried out of the hall, their joined steps creating a rhythmic thudding on the stone floor.

♠

Kira supervised the food arrangement, directing servants to move desserts from one side of the table to another with the precision of a military commander. Her attention was drawn to the entrance as Peek and Aboo returned, carrying a kicking and screaming Henry between them.

"I said put me down!" Henry protested, though he was clearly no match for the trolls' strength.

Kira approached the group, laughing at the sight. "When I said to fetch Henry, I meant to ask him to come here."

She reached under the present table and retrieved one of the wrapped packages. The trolls frowned as they gently set Henry down, looking disappointed that their game had ended.

"Time for presents!" Kira announced.

Peek and Aboo jumped up and down excitedly, their movements causing the tables to rumble and shake dangerously.

"I thought presents were tonight," Henry said, brushing himself off. "I haven't wrapped yours yet."

"I wanted you to have this early... so you could wear it tonight," Kira explained, then realized she had given away part of the surprise. "I mean..."

Henry smiled as she handed him the present. "Is it a falcon?" he asked, shaking and squeezing the package.

The soft feel of fabric was unmistakable to anyone who had ever received clothing as a gift. "Maybe a new dagger?"

"Just open it, will you?" Kira said impatiently.

Henry unwrapped the cloth and held up the green tunic. His initial reaction was one of shock - the gory coat of arms really did show pools of blood against the deep green fabric.

"It is green," he said carefully.

"Magnificent isn't it?" Kira said proudly. "We don't know anything about your family so..."

"I thought they might have been farmers, or woodsmen," Henry said, turning the tunic over and feeling the quality of the fabric. "The green is a nice shade and it is soft."

"I will be wearing the same tunic tonight," Kira announced. "I am proud to wear your colors."

Kira then dragged a huge package from under the table and placed it at the feet of the twin trolls. They shrieked in delight as they worked together to unwrap it. Henry leaned toward Kira and whispered his thanks.

"That was kind of you."

"I had dozens more made," Kira said, then handed him a package. "Tonight you get your own green troop after it is announced that we will be to ride into Romaland and teach both South and North Romaland a few lessons. Knights will be fighting to wear your colors after they hear about our quest."

♠

Owen, Dirk and Bart sat in the empty spectator stands after the jousting field had been cleared. Broken lances littered the ground like fallen soldiers, and the afternoon sun cast long shadows across the tournament grounds. Owen held the heavy purses of gold that Prince William had tossed at them, feeling their weight while his two companions watched with barely concealed greed.

"We leave in the morning," Owen announced, his weathered face showing the calculation of a man who had survived many dangerous ventures.

Dirk's eyes never left the purses. "We'll need to get tools, supplies..."

"And weapons," Bart added, unconsciously touching the hilt of his sword.

Owen studied his companions for a long moment. These two had served him well enough in the past, despite their obvious limitations. The kidnapping of Prince Alec had failed, but not through lack of courage. Still, entering the enchanted forest would require more than their usual rough work. He tossed one of the purses at the pair. Both men reached for it simultaneously, missing completely, and Dirk had to scramble to pick it up from the wooden planks of the spectator stand.

"I want the best weapons you can buy," Owen commanded, rising from his seat. The gold clinked as he secured the remaining purses in his belt.

As he prepared to leave, Owen turned back and frowned at his companions, who were already dividing their share of the coins. "If I'm going into that cursed forest with the two of you, I'm going heavily armed."

Dirk looked up from counting coins. "What about food? Supplies for the journey?"

"Use your heads," Owen replied with disgust. "We'll need everything if half the stories about that place are true. But weapons first - I'd rather starve than face whatever's in there defenseless."

Later, Owen inspected the supply cart with growing dismay. What should have been packed with provisions for a dangerous journey into unknown territory looked more like the leftovers from a village market. Dirk and Bart stood nearby, trying to look confident but failing miserably under his scrutiny.

"You plan on us eating screaming frogs or maybe tree bark?" Owen asked, his voice dangerously quiet.

Dirk pointed defensively to one of the baskets. "That one's half full of food."

"I tasted everything myself," Bart added proudly. "It's all fresh."

Owen shook his head in disgust. "Three of us for eight days, and half is gone after Bart's 'tasting'?" The two men shrugged, neither willing to take responsibility for the obvious shortage. Owen had seen enough. These fools would get them all killed if he didn't take charge completely.

"I'm giving you two hours to fill this cart with food," he commanded, stepping closer to emphasize his words. "And while you're gathering supplies, think carefully about who eats and who doesn't if there's any shortage on this journey."

Owen stalked away, leaving his companions to contemplate both the empty cart and his ominous threat. Bart turned to Dirk with genuine concern in his voice. "I would get to eat, right?"

Dirk shook his head in amazement at his partner's density. Without a word, he grabbed one side of the half-empty food basket and pointed for Bart to take the other side. They had work to do, and not much time to do it.

♠

Chapter 3 - Birthday Party

The great hall of Castle Latavia had been transformed into a magnificent celebration space that rivaled the grandest feast days of the kingdom. Enormous tapestries bearing the royal coat of arms hung from the stone walls, their rich blues and golds catching the flickering light of hundreds of beeswax candles placed in ornate iron sconces. The usual austere atmosphere of the hall had given way to something exciting and the smells were intoxicating.

Long oak tables groaned under the weight of the birthday feast. Roasted wild turkeys stuffed with herbs and chestnuts sat alongside massive haunches of venison, their skin crackling and golden. Platters of salmon lay arranged in intricate patterns, garnished with wild watercress and early autumn berries. The crowning item was a huge pig, with an orange in its mouth instead of the usual apple. The castle's bakers had outdone themselves with elaborate pastries shaped like knights and ladies, their crusts gleaming with egg wash and decorated with colored sugars that sparkled like jewels. The largest ones looked a lot like Kira and Henry.

Servants moved efficiently between the tables, adjusting the placement of silver goblets and ensuring that the ale barrels remained properly tapped. The kitchen had been working since dawn to prepare delicacies that would be talked about for months:

honey cakes dripping with golden sweetness, wheels of aged cheese from the castle's own dairy, and exotic spices traded from distant lands that filled the air with the scents of cinnamon and cardamom – and oranges; Kira's favorite fruit was the main ingredient in most of the little cakes for each guest. Each has a large "K" on it made with tiny beauty berries.

Near the high table, a group of traveling minstrels tuned their instruments – lutes, drums, and a small harp that caught the light beautifully. Their leader, a weathered man with clever eyes, tested a few notes while his companions warmed up with quiet practice runs. The music would need to be perfect for a royal celebration, especially one honoring both the princess and Henry.

But the most striking sight in the hall was not the feast or the decorations – it was the gathering of guests in their various states of reaction to the green tunics worn by the guests of honor. Princess Kira stood near the present table with obvious pride, wearing Henry's new colors with the gory coat of arms displayed prominently across her chest. The violent imagery of blood spurting from fallen knights made several noble ladies gasp and fan themselves dramatically. Fortunately, Grace had carefully put the coat of arms low on the tunic, so later, when Kira and Henry sat at the table, guest would not see it.

Henry stood beside her, equally resplendent in his matching tunic, though his expression showed a mixture of pride and bewilderment at the artistic choice. The bloody battle scene seemed even more vivid against the deep forest green of the fabric, and more than one knight had already made jokes about whether Henry planned to live up to such a fearsome reputation.

But perhaps the most remarkable sight was the twin trolls, Peek and Aboo, who had somehow been fitted with enormous versions of the same tunic. The sight of these massive, conjoined creatures wearing matching green garments with the ghastly coat of arms had caused quite a stir among the assembled nobility.

There was no way for Grace to hide the coat of arms on their massive tunics. Several children pointed and whispered, while their parents tried to maintain proper court etiquette despite their obvious fascination.

Grace, the tunic maker, hovered nervously near the edge of the crowd, still somewhat shaken from her earlier encounter with being lifted to hang decorations by the helpful but overzealous trolls. She watched anxiously as people examined her handiwork, particularly the challenging construction required for Peek and Aboo's unique physiology.

The hall gradually filled with the cream of Latavian society. Lords and ladies arrived in their finest garments, jewels glittering at their throats and wrists. Knights appeared in their dress uniforms, medals and honors polished to perfection. Even the castle's staff had been given new clothes for the occasion—all in Henry's green color, creating an atmosphere of celebration that touched every corner of the great hall.

Young Prince Alec ran between the tables, Henry's carefully carved horse figurine clutched tightly in his small hands as he galloped it along table edges and around chair legs. Queen Selina followed at a more dignified pace, her elegant blue gown a stark contrast to the greens dominating the color scheme. She smiled warmly at guests while keeping a careful eye on her energetic son.

"Happy birthday, dear Henry, happy birthday to you!" The drunken voices of Mark and James had begun the evening's entertainment, though their off-key singing and swaying suggested they had started celebrating well before the official festivities. The assembled crowd clapped politely, though several winced at the particularly discordant notes. Henry managed a gracious smile while Kira looked somewhat embarrassed by the early display. Peek and Aboo, however, began clapping enthusiastically and attempting to sing along, their booming voices drowning out the original performers entirely.

As the evening progressed, the feast began in earnest. Servants carved meat with practiced efficiency, filling trenchers with generous portions. The smell of roasted meats mixed with the yeast and hops of the flowing ale, creating an atmosphere of abundant celebration. Conversations grew livelier as cups were filled and refilled, though the unusual sight of talking trolls in formal wear continued to be a topic of whispered discussion.

The minstrels struck up a lively tune, and soon couples began forming for dancing. The music was traditional but spirited – reels and country dances that had been popular in Latavia for generations. Ladies' skirts swirled as they were spun by their partners, while the men demonstrated their agility and grace despite the substantial meal they had consumed.

Kira found herself in the unusual position of being asked to dance by several young nobles who came from far away; all curious about the fierce princess who had proven herself in battle. She accepted a few invitations but seemed more comfortable discussing military strategy than following dance steps. Her partners often found themselves listening to detailed descriptions of sword techniques rather than engaging in the usual court pleasantries. Many later commented that they hoped never to be engaged to such a difficult princess, even if the Kingdom of Latavia was an attractive alliance for any country.

Henry, meanwhile, had attracted attention for different reasons. His newly official knighthood made him an eligible bachelor in the eyes of many of the local court families, despite his humble origins. Several ambitious mothers pushed their daughters forward, hoping to catch the eye of the young knight who had the princess's obvious favor. Henry handled these attentions with characteristic politeness, though he seemed far more comfortable discussing horses and quest preparations than navigating the complex social dynamics of noble courtship. Kira had hinted that their quest might take them into Romaland and all he could think about was the village where he was born.

The twin trolls had become unlikely celebrities at the feast. Despite their fearsome appearance, their obvious joy and childlike enthusiasm charmed many of the guests. Children gathered around them, fascinated by their size and the way they moved as one unit. Peek and Aboo delighted in showing off their coordination, performing simple tricks and sharing stories of their adventures with Henry and Kira.

"Tell us about the poisoned snake bridge!" demanded one young lord, his eyes wide with excitement.

"No! Tell me about the monstrous mountain!" added a lady, her usual reserve forgotten in the face of such exotic entertainment.

The trolls launched into animated retellings of their adventures on a previous quest with Kira and Henry, their voices booming across the hall and drawing even more listeners. Their innocent pleasure in recounting tales of danger and heroism provided a stark contrast to their intimidating appearance, and soon they had quite an audience hanging on their every word.

Everyone was relieved to learn that the trolls now preferred roasted pig and turkey over humans.

As the evening wore on, the inevitable moment arrived for the formal presentation of the quest. A trumpet fanfare announced the entrance of King Phillip and Queen Selina, who took their places on the ornate thrones at the head of the hall. The king carried a silver platter bearing a single scroll, its wax seal gleaming in the candlelight.

The assembled crowd fell silent as King Phillip rose from his throne, his commanding presence immediately focusing all attention. He was an imposing figure even in celebration, his crown catching the light as he surveyed his subjects with obvious satisfaction.

"It is with great honor today that I wish Sir Henry and Princess Kira a happy birthday," he announced, his voice carrying easily through the hall.

The crowd erupted in applause, though Henry noticed some of the clapping seemed somewhat restrained. He caught a few exchanged glances between older knights and wondered if his elevation to knighthood was still a source of controversy among the established nobility. A few, especially, Mark and James didn't have the respect to contain their smirks.

King Phillip unwrapped the scroll and cleared his throat ceremoniously. "Now that they are thirteen, as tradition dictates, they will venture out on a quest to prove that they are brave, loyal, and bright."

He paused and gestured for Kira and Henry to join him near the thrones. Both young people moved forward with obvious excitement, though Henry's expression showed traces of nervousness alongside his anticipation.

"Of course, this is actually Henry's second quest. A few years back..." the king began, and then noticed the crowd's reaction. Several people sighed audibly, and even Queen Selina leaned forward to whisper something urgent in his ear.

"Maybe save that story for later tonight?" she suggested diplomatically. "I know how much they enjoy hearing it, but I think Henry will burst if you wait any longer."

The king looked down at the scroll and smiled, taking the hint. "Henry proved he was brave and loyal, but this quest will require far more. He will travel with the princess deep into the west and the enchanted forest."

The crowd's reaction was immediate and varied. Gasps of surprise mixed with nervous chuckles and scattered applause. The enchanted forest was legendary throughout Latavia, known more for mysterious disappearances than successful expeditions. It was where raptors were banned to live, never to be seen again. But most thought of it as a place that nobody wanted to go. There was nothing worth seeing. King Phillip raised his hand for silence.

"Please, please. It is a lot more dangerous than you think," he said, though his tone suggested he might not entirely agree with that assessment.

Mark, emboldened by ale and the festive atmosphere, turned to James and commented just loudly enough to be heard by nearby guests: "He might get a splinter from the enchanted trees."

"Or get kissed by the singing frogs!" James added with a laugh that carried across the suddenly quiet hall.

The crowd began laughing, the tension of the dangerous quest announcement dissolving into amusement at the perceived mildness of the challenge. But their laughter died quickly as Kira's face darkened with fury. In one swift motion, she drew her sword, the steel singing as it cleared its sheath. She approached Mark and James.

"Kira!" King Phillip's sharp command stopped her from advancing on the two knights, but the damage was done. The festive atmosphere had shattered like glass, replaced by uncomfortable silence and the gleam of naked steel.

Kira returned her sword to its sheath with obvious reluctance, her face burning with embarrassment and anger. Without a word, she turned and strode toward the great doors, her green tunic billowing behind her like a battle standard. The guests parted before her, none daring to meet her fierce gaze.

Henry quickly stepped forward and accepted the knighthood and quest scroll from the king's outstretched hand. "Thank you, Your Majesty," Henry said as he held the scroll that made his knighthood official. He gently traced his finger around his name, Henry, but there was no last name.

Henry looked up as Kira went through the door. She hadn't waited for him to receive the scroll, she didn't tap him on the shoulder with her sword, and there was no kiss or hug. He ran after her.

King Phillip watched them go with a mixture of concern and resignation. He had hoped the evening would end more peacefully, but Queen Selina placed a gentle hand on his arm, her expression sympathetic.

The minstrels, sensing the need to restore some semblance of celebration, struck up a more subdued tune. Conversations gradually resumed, though they were notably quieter and more careful than before. The feast continued, but the earlier joy had been replaced by a more cautious politeness.

Peek and Aboo, sensing the change in mood, gathered closer together and spoke in hushed tones. They had grown genuinely fond of both Henry and Kira during their adventures, and seeing their friends upset made them sad as well. Several guests approached them with questions about the quest and the enchanted forest, but the trolls seemed to have lost their earlier enthusiasm for storytelling.

As the evening wound down, servants began clearing tables and banking the great fires in the hearths. Mark and James, still flushed with ale and their own perceived cleverness, huddled together near one of the smaller tables, their voices carrying in the quieter hall.

"Well, that went better than I expected," Mark said with a satisfied grin, reaching for another cup of ale. "Did you see her face when everyone started laughing?"

James chuckled, swaying slightly on his feet. "Like a thundercloud ready to burst. I thought she might actually run us through right there in front of the king."

"The enchanted forest," Mark scoffed, shaking his head. "What's next, sending them to gather flowers in the gardens? At least they'll be out of our hair for a while."

"Assuming they come back at all," James added, then paused thoughtfully. "Though knowing our luck, they probably will. That girl's too stubborn to let a few trees get the better of her."

Mark glanced toward the great doors where Henry and Kira had disappeared. "Did you see the way Henry ran after her? Like a trained hound following his master!"

"More like a puppy dog," James corrected with a laugh. "Tail wagging, eager to please. 'Yes, Princess Kira, whatever you say, Princess Kira.' It's pathetic, really."

"A Romalander slave chasing after Latavian royalty," Mark said, his voice taking on a nastier edge. "Some things never change, no matter how many fancy titles you give them."

James nodded in agreement, raising his cup in a mock toast. "Here's to Sir Henry, the puppy knight, following his princess into the big scary forest."

♠

Henry rode up the familiar knoll on Augusta, finding Kira exactly where he expected - slashing at tree branches with her sword in violent, angry strokes. Each swing seemed to carry the weight of her frustration from the birthday party. He dismounted and approached cautiously, holding out the scroll that contained their quest orders.

"It is a quest," Henry said, trying to keep his voice reasonable. "Nobody has been to West Latavia for decades."

Kira stopped her assault on the innocent tree and knocked the scroll from his hand with a sharp blow. "For a good reason - it's on the way to nowhere. Nobody lives there."

"Exactly!" Henry's enthusiasm broke through despite her anger. "Think of how much land might be there for our villages to expand and farm. Think of what might be on the other side, what those roads might lead to..."

Kira's face hardened. "We have a real threat today - Romalanders. They need to be conquered, not ignored while we go chasing fairy tales in an empty forest."

Henry's own anger began to rise, and he bowed his head, fighting to control it. "Latavia conquered my birth country thirteen years ago. I was taken as a slave. When is it enough, Princess?"

"You are no more a Romalander than this horse," Kira said, reaching out to pet Augusta in what might have been meant as a reconciliatory gesture. "Tomorrow, I will as my father to give me a new quest."

But Henry pulled his horse away from her touch and mounted quickly. "This is my quest! Mine! I am going; with or without you!"

He wheeled Augusta around and rode off, leaving Kira alone on the knoll. She slumped down on a large rock, her anger deflating into something that looked almost like regret.

"Happy birthday, Kira and Henry," she whispered to the trail of dust.

Chapter 4 – The Beautiful Nesta

 The knight's quarters held a sanctity that the rest of the castle lacked. Thick wooden panels lined the walls, rich carpets muffled footsteps, and coats of arms hung in perfect formation like silent sentinels. In the center of the room, almost like an altar, stood a massive book on an ornate pedestal - the chronicle of every knight's quest for the past two centuries.

Henry stood before the open book, slowly turning its heavy pages. Each entry told of valor, of battles won and enemies defeated, of knights who had proven themselves worthy of remembrance. He found the section about their quest to save Prince Alec, reading Charles's careful script that detailed every challenge they had faced.

"There you are!" Kira's voice shattered the reverent quiet as she burst through the door.

Henry startled, then frowned at her irreverence in this sacred space. "Reading about our last quest," he said quietly.

"Now, that was a quest!" Kira declared, beginning to pace. "The twin trolls, poisoned snake bridge, monstrous mountain - real dangers, real enemies to fight."

Henry's finger traced the elegant writing. "I'm not even mentioned in the book."

"You weren't a knight," Kira said dismissively. "This is the knight's quest book. That was Charles's quest to save Alec. He was the knight in charge. But it will be your quest into West Latavia..."

"While you refuse to come with me," Henry interrupted, his voice thick with hurt. "I heard you calling it silly. What will it say in this book when I return?"

He slammed the heavy tome shut with a sound that echoed through the chamber like thunder. "For hundreds of years, knights will stand here and read about the quests. What will it say about me if my best friend ridiculed the quest if my best friend didn't even come with me?"

Henry turned toward the door, his shoulders set with wounded pride.

"It will say that Sir Henry valiantly led his troop through the Enchanted Forest..." Kira began, but when she looked up, Henry was already through the door and beyond hearing, leaving her alone.

♠

In the castle's east tower, Nesta sat at a wooden table covered with parchments, inkwells, and measuring instruments. Afternoon sunlight streamed through the tall windows, illuminating her work as she carefully traced the outline of Latavia's eastern border. Her grandfather's notes lay spread around her like a treasure map of knowledge accumulated over decades.

She paused in her work, setting down her quill and stretching her fingers. The intricate process of mapmaking required not just artistic skill, but mathematical precision that few possessed. Each measurement had to be exact, each landmark positioned with careful calculation of distance and elevation. Nesta often heard young men comment on her beauty, her style, her grace – but that didn't matter to her.

George the Geographer had been legendary in his field, but he had also been demanding. From the age of seven, Nesta had accompanied him on his expeditions, learning to read the landscape like others read books. She could estimate distances by studying shadows, determine elevation changes by observing water flow, and calculate travel times by analyzing terrain features.

"The land tells you everything, if you know how to listen," her grandfather had always said. "But you must be patient, observant, and above all, truthful in your recordings."

That truthfulness had sometimes put them at odds with nobles who preferred maps that flattered their territories or minimized their enemies' advantages. But George had insisted that accurate maps were more valuable than any amount of gold, and Nesta had learned to share his dedication to precision.

Her mother's influence had been different but equally important. As a former Romalander slave who had won her freedom through marriage, she had taught Nesta the value of adaptability and the importance of understanding both sides of any conflict. This dual heritage had made Nesta valuable as a mapmaker - she could move freely between North and South Romaland and Latavia, gathering information that others could not access.

A soft knock interrupted her thoughts. "Come in," she called, not looking up from her work. To her surprise, it was Henry who entered, carrying a leather satchel and wearing an expression of nervous determination. She had witness the whole drama at the birthday party and for a moment, she was jealous of the princess. Who wouldn't want a handsome knight chasing after her?

"Sir Henry," she said, rising and offering a graceful curtsy. "What brings you to my humble workspace?"

Henry seemed momentarily stunned by the sight of her surrounded by maps and instruments. The afternoon light caught the gold threads in her dark hair, and her concentration had given her cheeks a rosy flush that made her even more beautiful than usual.

"I... I wanted to ask about the maps of West Latavia," he managed. "For my quest."

Nesta smiled warmly, gesturing for him to join her at the table. "Of course! Though I must warn you, my grandfather's notes about the western territories are more legend than fact."

She pulled out a worn journal bound in cracked leather. "He explored the edges of the enchanted forest once, many years ago, but even he couldn't penetrate very far into the interior."

Henry leaned closer to examine the journal, and Nesta caught the scent of leather and horses that always seemed to cling to him. There was something endearingly earnest about his curiosity, so different from the arrogant assumptions of most nobles. She couldn't forget his face last night when he heard about the quest. The princess was disappointed, but Henry showed the same excitement that she felt.

"What did he find?" Henry asked, his finger tracing a rough sketch of towering trees.

"Strange things," Nesta replied, her voice dropping to almost a whisper. "He wrote about trees that seemed to move when he wasn't looking directly at them. Streams that changed course overnight. And sounds..."

"What kind of sounds?"

"Music, almost. As if the forest itself was singing." She paused, studying Henry's face. "Do you think I'm foolish for believing such stories?"

Henry shook his head seriously. "After everything Kira and I have seen on our travels, I've learned that the impossible is often just the improbable waiting to be discovered."

His response delighted her. Most people either dismissed her grandfather's stranger observations as the fantasies of an old man, or became so focused on the mysterious aspects that they ignored the practical information. Henry seemed to understand that both could be true simultaneously.

"You're not like the other knights," she observed, beginning to gather her materials. "They usually want to know about enemy positions and defensible terrain. You ask about the forest itself."

Henry looked surprised. "Isn't understanding the land itself the most important thing? You can't fight effectively in territory you don't comprehend."

"Exactly!" Nesta's eyes lit up with enthusiasm. "That's what grandfather always taught me. The land shapes everything - where people settle, how they travel, what they can grow, how they wage war. But so few leaders understand this."

She moved gracefully around the table, organizing her instruments with practiced efficiency. Henry watched, fascinated by the precision of her movements and the obvious expertise behind each action. He blushed for a moment. Nesta wore a long dress. It was sheer and seemed to be comfortable as it tightly hugged her curves.

"This astrolabe," she said, holding up a intricate brass instrument, "helps me determine exact positions using the stars. And this compass rose..." She showed him a beautifully decorated circular device. "It's not just for directions, but for calculating angles and distances between landmarks."

"How did you learn all this?" Henry asked, genuinely curious.

Nesta's expression grew more serious. "Necessity, mostly. When you're half Romalander in Latavia, you learn to make yourself indispensable. My skills keep me safe and fed, regardless of which kingdom currently controls the territory where I'm working."

The casual mention of her precarious position struck Henry. He had never considered how difficult her mixed heritage must make her life, caught between two often-hostile peoples.

"That must be... challenging," he said carefully.

"Less challenging than being a full Romalander slave," she replied with a slight smile. "At least I have value as a free person. My maps are sought after by nobles from both kingdoms."

Her words reminded Henry of his own complicated heritage, and he felt a sudden kinship with this beautiful, intelligent woman who also lived between worlds.

"I understand something of that difficulty," he said quietly. "Being Romalander-born but raised in Latavia."

Nesta set down her instruments and really looked at him for the first time. She had heard the stories, of course - the slave boy who had risen to knighthood through courage and loyalty. But seeing him now, she recognized something in his eyes that mirrored her own experience.

"It's lonely sometimes, isn't it?" she said softly. "Never quite belonging completely to either side."

Henry nodded, surprised by how accurately she had captured his feelings. "Princess Kira is... she's my closest friend, but sometimes I wonder if she sees me as Henry, or as her loyal Romalander."

"And what do you see when you look at yourself?" Nesta asked.

The question caught him off guard. "I... I'm not sure anymore."

Nesta moved closer, her voice gentle but serious. "I see someone who has earned his place through his own actions. Your birth doesn't define you, Henry. Your choices do."

The sincerity in her voice, combined with her proximity, made Henry's heart race. When had anyone ever spoken to him with such understanding, such respect for his struggles?

"Thank you," he managed. "That... that means more than you know."

Nesta smiled, and for a moment they stood in comfortable silence, two people who understood the complexity of divided loyalties and uncertain belonging.

"Perhaps," Nesta said eventually, "you could help me understand something about your quest. Why West Latavia? What does King Phillip hope to find there?"

Henry considered the question. "I think he hopes we'll find nothing. Empty land that poses no threat that requires no complex decisions or political maneuvering."

"But you hope for something different?"

"I hope to find... purpose, I suppose. A challenge, a discovery. Something that proves I'm worthy of the knighthood I've been given."

Nesta nodded thoughtfully. "In my experience, the most interesting discoveries come from the places we least expect to find them. West Latavia may surprise you both."

As Henry prepared to leave, gathering the maps Nesta had prepared for him, she caught his arm gently.

"My grandfather's notes mention more than just singing forests and moving trees. There are older stories, darker ones, about people who went into those woods and never returned."

"What kind of stories?"

"The kind that might be true," she said seriously. "Promise me you'll keep us safe."

Henry felt a warmth spread through his chest at her obvious concern. "I promise. I will protect you."

"If that is the case, I would like a tour of the village after I put away my things," she said as she started organizing the table. "Maybe you can meet me in the courtyard?"

Henry was speechless. He answered with eager nods, but as he left the tower room, Henry couldn't shake the feeling that his conversation with Nesta had changed something. For the first time, someone had looked past his origins and his usefulness to see simply Henry - not the former slave, not the grateful knight, but the person he was choosing to become; a protector.

He didn't notice Princess Kira watching from the courtyard below as he emerged from the tower, her face dark with an emotion she couldn't quite name. It was hard for her to see, but all she knew was they were way to close for her. One thing she did spot was that girl's hand on Henry's arm. Her own hand touched her sword.

♠

The morning sun cast a golden glow across the practice yard as Princess Kira and Charles, with wise and kind eyes, engaged in their usual sword training. Their blades rang out in a steady rhythm as they moved through familiar patterns.

Kira's mind kept drifting to the scene she had witnessed, and then, Henry emerging from the east tower with an expression she had never seen on his face before. It had been... peaceful, almost radiant, as if he had discovered something magical. The sight had filled her with anger.

"My first quest was shortly after you were born," Charles said, parrying one of Kira's strikes. "Your mother sent me south to gather wild flowers to put in your room."

"A wise ruler teaches her subjects how to obey an order," Kira replied, launching into a series of quick attacks.

But suddenly, Kira froze mid-strike, her attention caught by something across the courtyard. Charles almost ran her through with his sword as her guard dropped completely.

"What has caught your attention?" Charles asked, following her gaze.

There, walking arm in arm across the courtyard, was Henry with the most breathtakingly beautiful young woman Charles had ever seen. She had an exotic, fair beauty that seemed to make the very air around her shimmer. Her laugh tinkled like silver bells as Henry pointed out various features of the castle architecture, and she gazed up at him with obvious admiration.

"Ahhh... the beautiful Nesta, the geographer," Charles said with obvious admiration. "A great improvement over her grandfather George."

"Why is she so..." Kira struggled to find words for what she was seeing. There was something about Nesta's beauty that seemed almost otherworldly, but more troubling was the way she looked at Henry - and the way he seemed to bask in her attention.

"She is half Romalander," Charles explained. "Her father married a slave girl and Nesta spends some of the year in North Romaland with her mother's family."

Charles waved at the approaching pair, and they smiled warmly as they joined Kira and Charles. Nesta wore a sheer gown that seemed to float around her as she moved, making Kira acutely aware of her own practical tunic and the sweat stains from their sword practice. It was green. Kira wondered if she had chosen that for Henry.

"Might I have the pleasure, Princess, of introducing Nesta the geographer," Charles said with a gallant bow.

Nesta made a graceful curtsy that would have impressed even the court's most demanding etiquette master. "The pleasure is all mine, Princess Kira. Henry has told me so much about your legendary sword skills."

Kira found herself studying Nesta's attire with a critical eye, noting how Henry's gaze lingered on the young woman's elegant figure. "I never would have guessed that you were a geographer with that gown. How can you..."

Nesta's smile was both knowing and amused. "Trust me, when I am in the field, I look more like a horse than a lady. Henry is taking me into the castle today, so I thought the something green was a little more appropriate."

"The castle?" Kira's voice carried a sharp edge that made Henry shift uncomfortably. She noticed how Nesta's hand still rested possessively on Henry's arm.

Henry nodded eagerly, his face lighting up in a way that made Kira's stomach clench. "Nesta needs to look at the maps in your father's chancery again and Queen Selina was kind enough to invite us to lunch."

"I was so disappointed to hear you would not be joining us on Henry's quest," Nesta said, her voice carrying what seemed like genuine regret, though her eyes sparkled with something that looked almost like triumph.

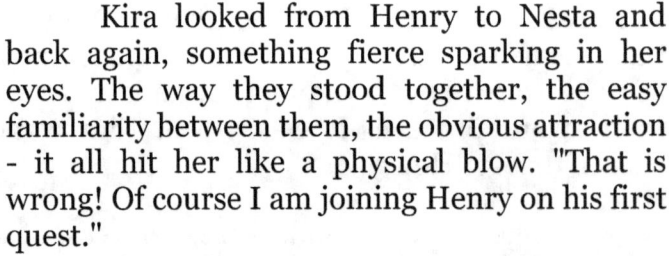

Kira looked from Henry to Nesta and back again, something fierce sparking in her eyes. The way they stood together, the easy familiarity between them, the obvious attraction - it all hit her like a physical blow. "That is wrong! Of course I am joining Henry on his first quest."

"But I thought..." Henry began, clearly confused by this sudden change, and perhaps a little disappointed that his time alone with Nesta would be interrupted.

"Charles has wisely convinced me that this quest's success is dependent upon my participation," Kira declared with finality, shooting a meaningful look at the older knight. "We leave early in the morning."

Without another word, Kira stormed off toward the castle, leaving Henry, Charles, and Nesta staring after her in bewilderment. She could hear Nesta's musical laugh behind her, followed by Henry's deeper chuckle, and it only fueled her anger.

Charles turned to Nesta with another gallant bow. "My dear Nesta, it is always a pleasure to see you. You are exactly what Henry's quest needs."

♠

Later that afternoon, in the great hall, Queen Selina, Nesta, and Henry sat at one of the long tables enjoying a fine lunch. The atmosphere was pleasant and relaxed until Kira entered the hall wearing Henry's green tunic with its gory coat of arms. Both Nesta and the Queen visibly winced at the sight.

"I see you started without me," Kira announced, her voice cutting through the gentle conversation like a blade.

Henry jumped to his feet. "We had no idea you would be joining us, Princess."

Nesta started to stand as well, but Kira motioned for her to remain seated as she pulled up a chair directly between Henry and the beautiful geographer. Servants quickly brought out a plate and wine for the princess.

"A warrior has to eat," Kira said, attacking her food with the same intensity she brought to sword fighting.

But eating didn't slow down her interrogation. She watched with growing irritation as Nesta delicately cut her meat into perfect small pieces while maintaining an animated conversation with Henry about the various mapping techniques she had learned from her grandfather.

"Are your troops prepared for the morning, Sir Henry?" Kira interrupted.

Henry smiled proudly, turning his attention from Nesta. "Yes, my Princess. They are packed and ready."

Kira's gaze shifted to Nesta like a hawk spotting prey. "And you, Nesta? I hope we are not hauling a bunch of gowns and slippers for you? The enchanted forest is no place for courtly fashion."

Nesta shook her head calmly, seemingly unperturbed by Kira's obvious hostility. "I bet I have less than Henry."

She reached across the table and patted Henry's hand in a gesture that seemed innocent enough. "Grandfather taught me that on journeys, our warriors are to protect, not serve."

Kira's eyes fixed on Nesta's hand resting on Henry's like a physical assault. The casual intimacy of the gesture, the way Henry didn't pull away, the slight flush that crept up his neck - it all confirmed her worst fears. With obvious anger, she grabbed food from her plate and stuffed it into her tunic pocket.

"I have no time for these silly luncheons," Kira declared, standing abruptly. "I need to prepare for our quest."

She left the hall with a loud stomp of her boots that echoed off the stone walls. Henry bowed his head and whispered sadly, "My quest."

Queen Selina looked between the door where Kira had disappeared and the obviously smitten young couple at her table. "Perhaps," she said gently, "we should spend the afternoon planning the practical aspects of your mapping expedition, Nesta."

Henry didn't hear the slam of hall walls. He didn't run after Kira. He didn't dig into the food. Instead, he waited for Nesta's answer to the queen's invitation.

Chapter 5 - The Quest

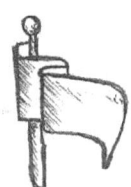 The next morning Henry and Nesta worked together to pack the cart, while Peek and Aboo helped by lifting them high over the wagon so they could rearrange items more efficiently. The sight of the conjoined twins hoisting people into the air had drawn a small crowd of curious castle folk.

Kira rode up on her horse, Julius, and quickly dismounted, her voice carrying across the courtyard with military precision. "Where are your troops, Sir Henry?"

Peek and Aboo immediately dropped Nesta and Henry into the cart with a soft thud, then turned to face Kira. They straightened their green tunics and stood at attention, their massive forms creating an impressive if unusual formation. Henry struggled out of the cart and joined them, forming a small but determined group.

"All here and accounted for, My Princess," Henry said formally, brushing hay from his hair.

Kira looked around the empty courtyard, noting several castle inhabitants watching from doorways and windows. "Them? Aboo and Peek are your whole green troop?"

"I'd rather have the two of them than a dozen of your knights," Henry replied with conviction, patting Peek on the arm.

As if summoned by his words, Mark and James appeared across the courtyard, singing loudly and clearly returning from a night of drinking. Their horses seemed to know the way home better than their riders, who swayed dangerously in their saddles.

"Reporting for your quest, Sir Henry," James slurred, attempting a salute that nearly toppled him from his mount.

"Ready for battle, Princess," Mark added before both men slid from their horses and collapsed to the ground unconscious, their snores immediately echoing off the cobblestones.

Several onlookers chuckled at the sight, while others shook their heads in disapproval. Nesta climbed out of the cart with a blanket and covered both sleeping knights with practiced efficiency.

"They were acceptable during my journey to map the forbidden lands earlier this year," Nesta said diplomatically, though her tone suggested she had low expectations.

Kira shook her head in disgust, and then turned to examine the trolls' tunics with a critical eye. "Where is your tunic with Henry's coat of arms?"

With surprising agility for creatures of their size, Peek and Aboo pivoted to show the backs of their tunics, which displayed the bloody battle scene in all its gory detail.

"We couldn't sleep looking at all that blood!" Aboo explained. His voice carried genuine distress.

"This is unacceptable, Sir Henry," Kira declared, her frustration mounting. "A troop of only two?"

Kira reached into her saddlebag and pulled out two more green tunics, tossing them onto the unconscious knights. "Toss them in the cart and tie up their horses to it. It is time to go."

♠

Peek and Aboo approached the unconscious knights with the enthusiasm of children given a new toy. They each grabbed a tunic and began the complex process of dressing the sleeping men.

"Arm goes here," Peek said, wrestling with Mark's limp form.

"No, that's a leg hole," Aboo corrected, tangling himself in James's tunic.

The twins' joined condition made the simple task monumentally difficult. When Peek tried to lift Mark's arm, Aboo was pulled sideways, causing James to roll over. When Aboo attempted to pull the tunic over James's head, Peek was yanked backward, and Mark's legs kicked reflexively.

"Maybe if we both work on one at a time?" Peek suggested.

They tried coordinating their efforts on Mark first, but their shared tunic meant they kept getting in each other's way. Aboo would reach for an arm while Peek grabbed a leg, and they'd end up twisted around each other like a massive green pretzel.

"This is harder than fighting the monstrous mountain," Aboo complained.

"At least the mountain didn't keep falling asleep," Peek agreed, as Mark's head lolled to one side just as they'd almost gotten the tunic over it.

Henry watched their struggles with growing amusement. "Perhaps if you work together like you do when you walk?"

The twins paused their efforts and looked at each other. "Oh! Like walking!"

They found their rhythm, moving in the coordinated dance they'd perfected over years of being joined. Soon they had both knights dressed in the green tunics, though Mark's was backward and James wore his inside out.

"Good enough," Kira declared impatiently. "Load them up."

The twins hefted the unconscious knights into the cart like sacks of grain, then secured their horses to the back. The whole process had drawn even more spectators, who applauded the trolls' efforts.

♠

Kira mounted her horse and began riding west, eager to leave behind the embarrassing spectacle and the knowing looks of the castle folk. Nesta and Henry quickly got on their horses while Peek and Aboo followed after their princess, keeping an eye on all the food in the cart.

The green troop had traveled hard through the morning, making good time on the well-maintained roads leading toward the western border. By afternoon they stood at the edge of the legendary enchanted forest, where ancient trees towered above them, their branches forming a canopy so thick that little sunlight penetrated to the forest floor.

Mark and James had awakened from their drunken stupor an hour earlier, their heads pounding and their memories foggy. They now wore their green tunics properly, though they grumbled constantly about their headaches and the humiliation of being dressed by trolls while unconscious.

"Road, trees, sky," Kira said impatiently, watching Nesta sketch in her notebook with meticulous detail. "How long does it take to draw that?"

"I've seen her take an hour to draw one river," James complained, holding his head.

"You should have seen her at the Monstrous Mountain," Mark added, thinking it was enough to be said about that.

Kira paced back and forth, her frustration growing with each minute. She couldn't shake the image of Henry and Nesta working so comfortably together earlier, or the way the geographer seemed to command his attention so effortlessly. "It is almost lunch and Aboo and Peek will certainly be hungry soon."

The twin trolls emerged from the forest at the sound of their names, each with frogs hanging from their mouths. The sight was both amusing and slightly disturbing, made worse by the satisfied expressions on their faces.

"I thought you were looking for firewood?" Kira asked, trying to hide her revulsion.

The trolls shook their heads in unison. Aboo managed to swallow his frog before answering guiltily, "There is no dead wood that we could find. But the noise..."

"The noise?" Henry asked, joining them.

"The frogs wouldn't stop screaming," Peek explained. "We thought eating them would make them quieter."

"Henry!" Kira called, eager to get moving and away from Nesta's methodical mapping.

Henry brought an empty basket and sack from the cart. "I was able to move things together and get these to hold the firewood and whatever else we find."

"Bring those and mount up," Kira ordered. "We'll go ahead and find a place to camp, while Mark, James and the trolls stay with her. Once we find it, we'll circle back and bring them to our camp."

Without waiting for a response, Kira mounted Julius and headed into the enchanted forest. Henry followed on Augusta, leaving the others to guard Nesta while she completed her mapping.

♠

Meanwhile, far to the north of their position, Owen, Dirk, and Bart approached the forest with their own agenda. The three Romalanders had made camp at the forest's edge the night before, and now prepared to enter the enchanted woods in search of the valuable timber Prince William desired.

Owen studied the tree line with a military eye, noting potential escape routes and defensive positions. Years of dangerous work had taught him to always plan for the worst.

"We'll make camp here tonight," Owen decided, dismounting from his horse near a stand of younger trees.

He walked back to their supply cart and frowned deeply. "Where is the food basket?"

Dirk and Bart looked at each other and shrugged with the casual indifference of men accustomed to disaster.

"I thought you put it in the cart," Dirk said.

"I told you to put it in there," Bart countered.

"I thought you said you had put it in there," Dirk replied, growing confused.

"Why would I tell you that I put it in there if I hadn't actually put it in there?" Bart asked, genuinely puzzled by the logic.

"Stop!" Owen barked, his patience exhausted. He had worked with these two long enough to know that letting them argue would accomplish nothing except give him a headache.

He tossed two hunting bags at their feet. "Go hunt for dinner and I'll make a fire and boil some water."

Dirk took the bag, and he and Bart headed into the forest, their voices already rising in a renewed argument about whose fault the missing food really was.

Owen shook his head as he watched them disappear into the trees. Working with idiots was exhausting, but Prince William paid well, and the promise of easy access to Latavia's western border made the job worthwhile. If they could establish a reliable route through the enchanted forest, future invasions would be far simpler than the costly direct assaults of previous wars.

He began gathering kindling, his mind already working on the tactical advantages the hidden road would provide. Latavia's defenses were all oriented toward their eastern and northern borders. A western approach through supposedly impassable enchanted lands would catch them completely unprepared.

♠

Kira and Henry rode deeper into the forest, the canopy growing thicker overhead until they moved through a world of green twilight. The air felt different here - charged with an energy that made the hair on their arms stand up.

"This place feels alive," Henry murmured, patting Augusta's neck as the horse grew increasingly nervous.

"Everything feels alive when you're looking for enemies," Kira replied, but her voice carried less conviction than usual. She too felt the strange presence surrounding them, as if unseen eyes watched their every move.

They rode in companionable silence for a while, following what appeared to be an old game trail deeper into the woods. For the first time since Nesta's arrival, Kira felt the familiar comfort of having Henry beside her without the distraction of the beautiful geographer's presence.

"I've been thinking about what you said," Henry said eventually. "About this being my quest."

Kira glanced at him, noting the serious expression on his face. "What about it?"

"You were right to be angry about my friendship with Nesta," he continued. "I was... distracted by her attention. It felt good to have someone think well of me for something other than my usefulness in battle."

"You think I don't think well of you?" Kira asked, her voice sharper than she intended.

Henry was quiet for a long moment. "Sometimes I wonder if you see me as Henry, or as your useful Romalander squire who happens to carry a knight's sword now."

The words hit Kira like a physical blow. She pulled Julius to a halt and turned to face him fully. "Is that really what you think?"

"I don't know what I think anymore," Henry admitted. "Nesta makes me feel like I could be someone important in my own right. Not just the former slave who proved himself useful."

Kira stared at him, a dozen emotions warring in her chest. Anger at his ingratitude, hurt at his doubt, fear at the thought of losing him - and underneath it all, something she couldn't quite name.

"You are important," she said finally. "You're the most important person in my life—well after my father, I guess, but if you can't see that, maybe Nesta is exactly what you deserve."

She spurred Julius forward, leaving Henry sitting alone on the trail, his face a mask of confusion and regret.

♠

An hour later, they had found a suitable clearing for lunch near a small stream and began preparing to return for the others. The tension between them remained thick, but practical concerns took precedence over personal conflicts.

"This will work," Kira said, dismounting near the water. "Good defensible position, fresh water, room for the cart."

Henry nodded, still subdued from their earlier exchange. "I'll mark the trail so the others can find it easily."

As they worked together to prepare the campsite, both were lost in their own thoughts. Neither noticed the tiny changes in their surroundings - the way certain branches seemed to bend toward them, closer and closer, or how the stream's bubbling grew more musical, almost like laughter. The enchanted forest was beginning to take notice of its visitors, curious.

Chapter 6 - Screaming Frogs

The morning air hung thick with mist as Bart and Dirk stumbled back into Owen's camp, each carrying bulging sacks that writhed and shrieked with an unholy cacophony. The sound was enough to wake the dead, and certainly enough to make Owen clap his weathered hands over his ears as his two companions approached.

"By all the saints in heaven, what is that ungodly noise?" Owen bellowed, having to shout to be heard over the din.

Bart hefted his sack higher, wincing as whatever was inside continued its vocal assault. "You said to bring back dinner, so we brought back dinner!" he called back, though even he looked miserable holding the screaming burden.

"We tried to shut them up," Dirk added miserably, blood still seeping through the makeshift bandage on his arm from their earlier encounter with Princess Kira. "But they just get louder when you poke them!"

Owen strode over and peered into one of the sacks. His eyes widened at the sight of the enormous frogs within – each one easily the size of a fat rabbit, with bulging eyes and throats that pulsed with each ear-splitting croak. They were unlike any frogs he'd ever seen, with mottled green and brown skin that seemed to shimmer with an almost metallic sheen.

"These are no ordinary marsh frogs," Owen muttered, reaching into the sack despite the increased volume of protest from its occupants. "Look at the size of them!"

He grabbed one of the creatures by its hind legs and pulled it from the bag. The frog's screaming reached new heights of indignation as Owen held it up for inspection. Its mouth gaped wide enough to swallow a man's fist, revealing rows of tiny sharp teeth that glinted in the morning light.

"Perhaps if we silence them properly..." Owen said, drawing his sword with his free hand.

"Don't!" Dirk shouted, but it was too late.

Owen brought his blade down toward the frog's neck with the practiced efficiency of a man who had dispatched countless enemies. But instead of the clean cut he expected, the moment his steel touched the creature's skin, it exploded.

The blast knocked Owen backward, covering him from head to toe in sticky frog innards. Chunks of green and brown flesh dripped from his hair, his beard, his clothes. The explosion had been so sudden and complete that nothing remained of the frog larger than Owen's thumb.

Bart, who had seen this performance before, had wisely ducked behind a tree. "That's why we didn't tell you right away," he called out sheepishly.

Owen stood there dripping, his sword still raised in the air, looking like he'd been dunked in a vat of swamp water. "Why didn't you warn me before I grabbed the cursed thing?" he snarled, flinging bits of frog off his blade.

"Why do you think we're covered in blood?" Dirk replied, gesturing to the state of his and Bart's clothing. Both men looked like they'd been splattered with paint from head to toe. "Bart kept trying to kill them until he finally understood what happens."

Owen turned his glare on Bart, who was still peeking out from behind his tree. "How many did you have to explode before you figured out they weren't normal frogs?"

Bart and Dirk exchanged a look and shrugged in unison – a gesture that had become their standard response to Owen's increasingly frequent questions about their intelligence.

"Maybe a dozen or so," Dirk admitted. "But we think if we boil them alive, they might not explode the same way."

Owen walked over to their campfire, his boots squelching with each step, leaving a trail of frog debris. He grabbed their iron pot and filled it with water from their dwindling supply. "There's an old wives' tale about cooking frogs," he said, his voice taking on the tone of a man explaining something to children. "If you drop a frog into boiling water, it will jump out immediately. But if you put it in cool water and heat it slowly, it won't notice until it's too late to escape."

Both Dirk and Bart nodded eagerly, though their expressions suggested they didn't entirely understand the principle behind it.

Owen set the pot over the fire and gestured for them to add a few of the screaming creatures to the cool water. The frogs seemed content enough, floating peacefully as the water began to warm. Their screaming died down to what might charitably be called a murmur.

"Same principle applies to working with you two idiots," Owen continued, wiping frog guts from his chin. "Your stupidity creeps up so slowly that I don't notice how bad it's getting until it's too late and something explodes in my face."

Despite his harsh words, there was something almost companionable about their morning routine. They had been working together long enough that even Owen's insults had taken on the comfortable rhythm of an old married couple's bickering.

♠

Meanwhile, several chains to the south, the green troop had ridden hard through the morning. The ancient trees of the enchanted forest loomed around them like cathedral pillars, their branches weaving together high overhead to create a living ceiling that filtered the sunlight into shifting patterns of gold and green.

Princess Kira heard them coming, ran into the road and raised her hand. "Water your horses and then come to the clearing ," she commanded.

The sight of fresh water was a blessing after their long ride through the thick forest air. Mark and James dismounted with visible relief, leading their horses to the stream's edge where the animals drank gratefully.

Peek and Aboo, having no horses to tend, immediately lumbered over to a massive oak tree and collapsed in its shade. Within moments, their synchronized snoring echoed through the clearing like a pair of mismatched bellows, causing several birds to take flight in alarm.

Henry and Nesta found a comfortable spot on a smooth boulder overlooking the stream. The morning ride had been pleasant despite the urgency of their quest, and Henry found himself stealing glances at the beautiful mapmaker as she pulled a worn leather notebook from her tunic.

"Already working?" Henry asked, settling beside her on the warm stone.

Nesta shook her head, her dark hair catching the dappled sunlight. "This area has been mapped well enough by my grandfather. I'm reading his notes about West Latavia – about what we might encounter deeper in the forest."

Henry leaned closer to examine the pages, catching the faint scent of lavender and parchment that seemed to follow Nesta wherever she went. The notebook was filled with her grandfather's careful script, interspersed with detailed sketches of plants, animals, and geographical features.

"Listen to this," Nesta said, running her finger along a particular passage. "The enchanted forest is reported to be filled with mythical creatures: screaming frogs, fierce fireflies, and gripping vines." She looked up at Henry with a mixture of curiosity and amusement. "I'm wondering how a firefly can be fierce, and how exactly does a frog scream?"

Henry laughed, covering his ears in an exaggerated gesture of protection. "I think I could conquer a screaming frog easily enough."

Nesta pulled his hands down from his ears, her touch sending an unexpected warmth up his arms. Her laugh was like silver bells chiming. "But how would you fight a firefly? They're so small and quick!"

From across the clearing, Princess Kira noticed the cozy pair and shook her head in disgust. There was something about the way they sat so close together, the way Nesta's laughter made Henry's face light up, that twisted uncomfortably in her chest.

Henry, oblivious to Kira's observation, jumped up from the boulder and drew his sword with theatrical flair. "Like this!" he declared, swinging his blade through the air in elaborate patterns, chasing imaginary fireflies in wild swooping arcs.

His performance was so enthusiastic and ridiculous that Nesta rolled off the boulder, laughing so hard she could barely breathe. Her mirth was infectious, waking Peek and Aboo from their nap. The twin trolls sat up, stretching and grinning at Henry's antics.

"We want to play!" Peek called out eagerly.

"What is the game?" Aboo added, his massive frame already rising from the ground.

The sight of the trolls preparing to join Henry's imaginary battle with flying insects was too much for Kira's patience. She strode over to the group and shouted sharply, "Enough of your child's play! Mount up − I want to be deep in the forest by sunsest."

Her tone brooked no argument, but Henry couldn't help noticing how her gaze lingered disapprovingly on Nesta, who was still picking grass from her hair and trying to compose herself after her fit of giggles.

As the group prepared to depart, Nesta carefully tucked her grandfather's notebook back into her tunic. "Your grandfather sounds like he had quite the imagination," Henry said quietly as they walked toward their horses.

"That's what most people say," Nesta replied, her voice thoughtful. "But he was never wrong about the lands he mapped. If he says there are screaming frogs in these woods, then I suspect we'll hear them soon enough."

♠

Back at Owen's camp, the morning had progressed with its own peculiar challenges. The three Romalanders had managed to consume their unusual breakfast of boiled screaming frogs, though the taste left much to be desired. The creatures had indeed proved less explosive when cooked slowly, but their flavor was indescribably awful – like marsh water mixed with rotting fish.

"Next time, I'm catching my own lunch," Dirk complained, picking bits of frog meat from between his teeth.

"Next time, you'll eat what you're given and be grateful for it," Owen replied, though he had to admit the meal had been less than appetizing. He stood up and surveyed the thick forest around them. "Pack up the gear and move the cart over to that stand of young trees."

He pointed toward a grove of saplings in the distance, their tender green leaves catching the morning light. "Young trees are easier to uproot. We can cut through their roots more easily and dig them up without breaking every tool we have. We should have the cart filled by noon and be on our way home."

Owen clapped Bart on the shoulder, though not gently. "While Dirk and I work on the trees, you gather enough frogs to last us for the journey back to Romaland. And try not to explode half of them this time."

The wind picked up suddenly, blowing from the west and sending the ashes from their campfire swirling into their faces. All three men jumped up, coughing and spitting, rubbing ash from their stinging eyes.

"The sooner we get out of this cursed place, the better," Bart muttered, still blinking away tears from the ash.

Owen nodded grimly. "These woods feel wrong. The sooner we fill that cart with Prince William's precious timber and return to civilized lands, the happier I'll be."

As they broke camp and prepared for their work, none of them noticed the way the trees seemed to lean inward slightly, as if listening to their conversation. The forest had been watching them since they arrived, and it was not pleased with their intentions.

♠

Hours later, as the sun climbed higher through the canopy, the green troop continued their journey deeper into the enchanted forest. The path had become increasingly narrow and overgrown, forcing them to ride single file through corridors of ancient bark and hanging moss.

Nesta had taken to riding on the shoulders of Peek and Aboo, using their height advantage to get a better view of the surrounding terrain for her mapping. The trolls seemed delighted to have her as a passenger, taking turns lifting her up so she could see over particularly dense patches of undergrowth.

"A little to the left," she directed, pointing toward a distant mountain peak visible through a gap in the trees. "Perfect! Now hold steady while I take some measurements."

She pulled out a brass astrolabe and began calculating distances and elevations, her trained eye reading the landscape like a familiar book. The trolls remained perfectly still, understanding the importance of her work even if they didn't fully comprehend what she was doing.

Mark and James, bringing up the rear, were having their own adventure with the local wildlife. Both knights had managed to catch several of the screaming frogs that seemed to populate every stream and pond in the forest. The creatures were even larger than the ones Owen's group had encountered, and considerably more vocal about their captivity.

"Can't you make them shut up?" James complained, holding his squirming sack at arm's length as if it contained venomous snakes.

"I've tried everything except killing them," Mark replied, his own sack writhing violently. "And after what happened to that other fellow, I'm not about to try that approach."

They had been unlucky enough to witness one of Bart's earlier attempts at frog-silencing, watching from a safe distance as the creature exploded in a shower of green muck. The memory was enough to make both knights handle their captives with considerably more care.

Two particularly large frogs managed to escape Mark's sack, hopping frantically toward the safety of the underbrush. After hopping for what seemed like days, the frogs came out of the bushes and screamed when they saw the twin trolls.

Peek spotted source of the noise and reached down to scoop it up with one massive hand. Aboo grabbed the other.

"Ouch!" the frog protested in a clear, distinctly annoyed voice.

Peek dropped the creature in shock, staring down at it with wide eyes. "You can talk?"

The frog – who would later introduce himself as Freddy – dusted himself off with as much dignity as a large green amphibian could muster. "Of course we can talk. Most creatures in this forest can, if humans would bother to listen instead of trying to eat us immediately."

Aboo leaned down to get a better look at the talking frog. "Then why are you called screaming frogs instead of talking frogs?"

Freddy fixed him with a look that suggested the answer should be obvious. "Probably because humans usually try to eat us before we can get a word in. You people aren't exactly known for your patience when it comes to conversation with your dinner."

Peek, his curiosity overcoming his caution, picked up Freddy again. "Well, if you can talk, maybe we can work something out..." Aboo had already figured things out and put his frog into his mouth.

Peek opened his mouth wide, displaying a truly impressive set of teeth, but before he could continue, Freddy let out a scream that made their earlier vocalizations seem like whispered lullabies. The sound was so piercing, so absolutely ear-splitting, that Peek immediately dropped the frog and covered his ears in pain.

"Wait, wait!" Freddy called out as Aboo bent down to pick him up in turn. "Let's talk about this like civilized beings!"

Chapter 7 - The Enchanted Forest

The acrid smell of ash filled Owen's nostrils as he wiped soot from his stinging eyes. The wind had picked up again, swirling the remnants of their morning campfire directly into the faces of the three Romalanders. Bart spat repeatedly, trying to clear the taste of charcoal from his mouth while Dirk rubbed his eyes with his sleeve, only making them redder.

"The sooner we get out of this cursed place, the better," Bart muttered, still blinking away tears from the ash.

Owen surveyed the grove of young saplings they had selected for harvest. The tender trees swayed in the morning breeze, their pale green leaves catching the filtered sunlight that managed to penetrate the forest canopy. These would be much easier to uproot than the massive ancient trees that dominated most of the enchanted forest.

"Pack up the gear and move the cart over to that stand of young trees," Owen commanded, pointing toward the grove. "Young trees are easier to cut the roots and dig up. We should have the cart filled by noon and be on our way home."

He clapped Bart on the shoulder, though not gently. "While Dirk and I work on the trees, you gather enough frogs to last us for the journey back to Romaland. And try not to explode half of them this time."

Bart nodded reluctantly, still nursing the various cuts and burns he had sustained during his previous encounters with the volatile amphibians. The screaming frogs of the enchanted forest were unlike any creatures he had ever encountered in normal lands.

The three men set to work with their axes and shovels, approaching the first cluster of saplings with the confidence of experienced woodsmen. Owen selected a particularly straight specimen about as thick as a man's arm and began chopping at its base while Dirk worked to clear the undergrowth around its roots.

But something was wrong. As Owen's axe bit into the bark, a sound escaped from the tree that was distinctly unlike the usual crack and splinter of cut wood. It was more like a gasp, high-pitched and startlingly human.

"Did you hear that?" Dirk asked, pausing in his digging.

Owen wiped sweat from his forehead. "Hear what? Just keep digging."

But as Dirk's shovel cut through the earth around the sapling's roots, more sounds emerged from the grove around them. Whispers seemed to rustle through the leaves, though there was no wind. The very air felt charged with an energy that made the hair on their arms stand up.

Bart returned from his frog-hunting expedition earlier than expected, his face pale and his hands empty of the usual sacks of screaming prey.

"The trees attacked me," he announced breathlessly.

Owen looked up from his work and laughed harshly. "I think you've been listening to the frogs too long. I heard they can make you crazy."

"That would explain it," Bart replied, rubbing his leg where several scratches showed through his torn pants. "I thought I heard them talking to me, too."

"The frogs?" Owen asked, returning to his chopping.

"No, the trees. It sounded like they called me a murderer. I've never run so fast..." Bart's voice trailed off as he looked nervously at the saplings they were harvesting.

Dirk managed to dig up another sapling and toss it into the cart, its roots still trailing clods of dark earth. "Didn't hear a word out of this one," he said, though his voice carried less conviction than his words.

Owen and Dirk shared a look and laughed at Bart's obvious terror, but their laughter died quickly as a low rumble began to emanate from the ground beneath their feet. The saplings around them began to sway without any wind, and the whispers in the leaves grew louder and more distinct.

"Murderers," the voices seemed to say. "Child killers."

This time, all three men heard it clearly.

♠

Far to the south, Henry reached over and gently patted Kira's horse as they rode side by side through the dappled sunlight of the forest path.

"I see you selected Julius this time instead of April," Henry observed, running his hand along the horse's neck.

Kira leaned over in her saddle to study the horse more closely. The animal turned its head and winked at her with surprising intelligence.

"That is his name?" she asked, somewhat surprised.

Henry nodded. "He is the brother of Athena, who died on our last quest at the poisoned snake bridge."

A shadow of sadness crossed Kira's face as she remembered the noble horse that had carried them so far before succumbing to the bridge's venom. She had tried not to form attachments to the horses from the royal stables, treating them more as tools of war than as companions.

"I never think about their names," she admitted quietly. "I tell the squire to saddle up something for me to ride. I try not to get close to them."

Henry leaned forward to stroke his own horse's mane affectionately. "I can't imagine not being close to Augusta. Gus is somebody I can talk to about my troubles."

Kira's laugh had a bitter edge to it. "Troubles? What troubles could you possibly have?"

Henry considered this for a moment, then decided to play it safe rather than delve into the complex emotions surrounding his heritage and uncertain place in the kingdom.

"For one thing, I think we are lost," he said instead.

"Lost?" Kira scoffed. "We are going west. All we have to do is turn around and go home."

She looked behind her, frowning as she tried to spot the sun through the thick canopy. "The sun was at our back a few moments ago."

"Exactly," Henry agreed, his voice taking on a more serious tone. "Since we have entered this thick forest, we can no longer see the sun at our back. I was watching the mountains to the north of Romaland that were to our right. I can't see them anymore either."

They both dismounted, leading their horses as Henry continued his explanation. "If we get turned around for any reason, we won't know which way to go."

Kira pulled some red rope from her saddlebag, her expression determined but tinged with something that might have been uncertainty. "Before there were map makers like your precious Nesta, people used this method to find their way back."

She approached a massive oak tree that stood like a pillar beside what appeared to be the main path through the forest. The tree was ancient and enormous, its trunk easily twenty feet in circumference, its branches reaching so high that the top disappeared into the green canopy above.

"You keep the red rope on your right when going somewhere, then collect it on your left coming back," Kira instructed, beginning to wrap the rope around the tree's gnarled bark. "Simple!"

Henry joined her at the massive tree, helping her secure the rope around its wide girth. The bark felt strange under his hands – warm, almost pulse-like, as if something alive moved beneath the surface.

As Henry completed tying the knot, the ground beneath their feet began to rumble.

It started as a low vibration that they felt more than heard, rising up through the soles of their boots and into their bones. The rumbling grew stronger, accompanied by a sound like distant thunder that seemed to come from all directions at once.

The wind began to blow with supernatural force, whipping through the branches above them and causing the massive tree to sway despite its size. Kira and Henry struggled to maintain their footing as the earth beneath them started to shift and crack.

"Henry!" Kira shouted, but her voice was lost in the growing roar of wind and groaning wood.

Thick roots erupted from the forest floor like enormous serpents, moving with purpose and intelligence that defied everything Henry and Kira thought they knew about the natural world. The roots wrapped around their legs before either of them could react, their grip firm but not crushing.

These weren't ordinary roots – they moved with deliberate intent, as if guided by some vast intelligence. More vines descended from the canopy above, winding around their arms and torsos as they were lifted from the ground.

Kira struggled against the restraints, her warrior instincts demanding action even as her rational mind tried to process what was happening. Her raptor blood surged, demanding she spread her wings and fly free, but the ancient laws bound her wings as surely as the vines bound her body.

"Henry!" she called out again, but he was already being pulled upward into the canopy, hundreds of feet above the ground.

They rose through layers of branches and leaves, past startled birds and bewildered squirrels, higher and higher until the forest floor became a distant green carpet below. The sensation was dreamlike and terrifying, as if they were being drawn into the very heart of the forest's mystery.

As they ascended, Henry's head struck a particularly thick branch, and darkness claimed his consciousness. Moments later,

Kira's world went black as well when her skull connected with an enormous limb.

When consciousness finally returned to Kira, she found herself hanging upside down, suspended by enchanted vines in a circle of enormous trees. But these weren't just trees – they had faces. Ancient, wise, and unmistakably alive.

Three massive faces studied her with expressions ranging from maternal concern to outright hostility. Each face was carved into the bark of a different tree, but the features moved and shifted with life and intelligence. The faces were distinctly feminine, with flowing hair made of hanging moss and eyes that glowed with an inner light.

"This one is waking up," said the first face in a voice that sounded hauntingly familiar. For a moment, Kira could have sworn it sounded like her mother's voice, but that was impossible. Her mother was dead, and Kira had been responsible for her death.

Kira's eyes snapped fully open, her training keeping her alert despite the disorientation of hanging upside down hundreds of feet in the air. She quickly assessed her situation – bound by vines, suspended in what appeared to be a natural amphitheater formed by the crowns of ancient trees.

"Where are our children?" demanded the angriest of the three faces, leaning so close that Kira could smell earth and musty leaves on her breath. The face's expression was one of grief mixed with fury, like a mother who had lost everything she held dear.

Princess Kira had faced armies, conquered the monstrous mountain, crossed the poisoned snake bridge, and even made friends with twin trolls, but nothing had prepared her for talking trees that held her prisoner in their branches. As she hung there, defenseless and at their mercy, she realized this quest had become something far more dangerous than anyone had imagined.

The tree that had spoken identified herself as Francis, and she was clearly the most volatile of the three. Her bark was darker than the others, scarred with what looked like old wounds, and her eyes burned with an intensity that made Kira's warrior blood run cold.

"We know what you humans do," Francis continued, her voice rising with each word. "You come into our forest with your axes and saws, cutting down our children without thought or care. You see us as nothing more than timber for your buildings and fuel for your fires."

The second face, gentler but no less ancient, introduced herself as Ida. Her bark was smoother, marked with the silver scars of old lightning strikes, and her voice carried the weight of centuries. "We have watched your kind for generations," Ida said sadly. "Some of you come seeking knowledge or shelter, and those we help by giving you our banches. But others come with destruction in their hearts, and those we cannot allow to leave."

The third face, Mabel, seemed to be the eldest of the three. Her features were carved deep into bark so old it had turned nearly black, and when she spoke, her voice carried the authority of someone who had seen the rise and fall of kingdoms. "Tell us," Mabel said, her tone measured but dangerous, "what have you done with our children? The young ones who grew in the grove to the north? They were there yesterday, and today they are gone."

Henry stirred to consciousness nearby, also suspended upside down by the enchanted vines. He blinked in confusion, trying to process the sight of the massive tree faces surrounding them.

"I don't understand," Henry managed to say. "What children?"

Mabel's attention turned to him, and her expression softened slightly. "This one has the look of a sapling himself," she observed. "Young and still growing."

"But he travels with her," Francis pointed out accusingly, gesturing toward Kira with a movement of her branches. "And she bears the weapons of a destroyer."

Kira found her voice at last. "We haven't harmed any children," she said firmly. "We're on a quest draw maps, only maps with a Romanlander."

"Romalanders," Ida repeated thoughtfully. "Yes, we have seen them in our forest. Three men with sharp tools and cruel intentions."

Francis's expression grew even darker. "They took our children! Cut them down with axes and saws, loaded them into a cart like they were nothing more than firewood!"

As the three ancient trees spoke, Kira began to understand the magnitude of what had happened. The Romalanders – Owen, Dirk, and Bart – had not just been gathering timber. They had been destroying the children of these ancient, sentient trees.

"Close your eyes," Ida commanded suddenly. "All of you, close your eyes."

Kira, Henry, and even Francis and Mabel closed their eyes as commanded. Immediately, Kira's mind was filled with visions – images that seemed to flow directly from the consciousness of the trees themselves.

She saw Owen, Dirk, and Bart working with their axes and shovels in a grove of young saplings. She watched in horror as they cut down tree after tree, tossing the small bodies into their cart with casual indifference. She could feel the pain and terror of the saplings as they were severed from their roots, hear their earthy screams as they were torn from the land that had nurtured them.

"Owen," Kira breathed, recognizing the leader of the group. "I know him. He and his gang were the ones Peter used to kidnap my little brother, Prince Alec, years ago."

Henry opened his eyes, looking confused. "I didn't see anything."

Mabel studied him with interest. "You are a pollinator," she explained. "Only fruit-bearing trees can share the sight. You are meant to spread seeds and encourage growth, not to witness destruction."

Francis leaned closer to Mabel. "We should probably weed out this extra pollinator. He serves no purpose here. He is a Romalander."

"No!" Kira struggled against her bonds, the vines holding her swaying with her movement. "I need Henry to find these villains and replant your saplings. Your children might not be dead yet – if we can get them back into the ground quickly enough, some might survive."

The three tree mothers moved their massive heads close together, their branches intertwining as they communicated in ways that went beyond human understanding. The wind picked up around them, and Kira could hear what sounded like the voices of hundreds of trees throughout the forest, all contributing to some vast arboreal council.

Finally, their conference ended, and the three faces turned back to their captives.

"The grove has decided," Ida announced solemnly. "We will release you for now. You have until the sun sets tomorrow to find our children and return them to the earth where they belong."

Mabel's voice carried the weight of absolute authority. "Find our children and save them, and you will live. Fail, and you will join them in death."

Francis added with barely contained fury, "And if you betray our trust, if you try to escape without fulfilling your promise, we will hunt you through every forest in every land until justice is served."

The vines began to lower Kira and Henry slowly, but when they were still about halfway down from the canopy, the ancient trees simply released them. Both young people fell the remaining distance to the forest floor, landing hard among the fallen leaves and soft earth.

The impact drove the breath from their lungs and sent shooting pains through their bodies, but nothing seemed to be broken. As they lay gasping on the ground, unconsciousness claimed them both once more, this time bringing not the violent darkness of injury, but the deep, restorative sleep that the forest itself seemed to impose upon them.

Above them, the ancient faces watched with expressions of grim hope. Their children of the forest had been taken, but perhaps – just perhaps – these two young humans could bring them home. But they were only human.

Chapter 8 - A River or the Sea

The morning mist clung to the enchanted forest floor like a wet blanket as consciousness slowly returned to Princess Kira. She found herself lying on a bed of soft moss beneath an ancient oak, with no memory of how she had arrived there. The last thing she remembered was hanging upside down from the vines of the talking trees, their ancient faces studying her with expressions ranging from maternal concern to outright fury.

Henry stirred beside her, groaning as he sat up and rubbed his head. His dark hair was tousled with leaves and small twigs, and his tunic bore the green stains of crushed moss and bark. "My head feels like it was used as a battering ram to storm the castle doors," he muttered, wincing as he touched a tender spot behind his ear.

Kira pushed herself upright, her warrior instincts immediately alert despite her disorientation. The forest around them seemed different somehow – quieter, more watchful. Shafts of golden sunlight filtered through the canopy above, creating dancing patterns on the forest floor. But something was wrong.

"Henry," she said, her voice sharp with concern. "Where are our swords?"

They both looked around frantically, searching the moss and fallen leaves. Their weapons were nowhere to be seen – not beside them, not hanging from nearby branches, not even gleaming in the distance where they might have fallen.

Henry spotted his sword first, its familiar leather-wrapped hilt visible nearly fifty yards away, wedged between the roots of a massive pine tree. Kira's blade lay even farther in the opposite direction, its silver pommel catching the morning light from beneath a tangle of flowering vines.

"How did they get so far away?" Henry asked, his voice filled with genuine puzzlement. "And why don't I remember anything after the trees showed us those visions?"

Kira frowned, pressing her fingers to her temples as if she could squeeze the missing memories from her skull. The last clear image in her mind was Francis, the angriest of the tree mothers, leaning close with breath that smelled of earth and ancient wood. Everything after that was a blur of green darkness and whispered voices.

"The trees," she said slowly. "They must have done something to us. But why separate us from our weapons?"

As they retrieved their swords, checking the blades for damage and ensuring the leather bindings were still secure, both warriors felt the weight of unanswered questions. The enchanted forest had proven far more mysterious and dangerous than either had anticipated, and they were no closer to finding Owen and his companions.

"At least we still have the horses," Henry said, pointing toward a nearby clearing where Julius and Augusta grazed peacefully on sweet grass. The animals showed no signs of distress or enchantment, which provided some small comfort.

Kira sheathed her sword and approached Julius, running her hand along his neck to check for any signs of harm. The horse whickered softly and nuzzled against her shoulder, as if trying to provide reassurance. "The trees said we had until sunset tomorrow to find their children and return them to the earth," she said. "We've already lost precious time."

They mounted quickly and set off through the forest, following what appeared to be an old game trail that wound deeper into the western reaches of the enchanted woods. The morning air was crisp and clean, filled with the scents of wildflowers and pine sap, but beneath the natural beauty lay an undercurrent of tension that made both riders constantly glance over their shoulders.

♠

The trail led them steadily westward for several hours, winding through groves of silver birch and stands of towering oaks whose trunks were so massive that six men holding hands could not have encircled them. Occasionally they passed clearings where wildflowers grew in impossible profusion – blues and purples and golds that seemed to glow with their own inner light.

"This place is beautiful," Henry said as they paused to water their horses at a crystal-clear stream. "It's hard to believe anything evil could happen here."

Kira nodded, but her expression remained guarded. "Beautiful things can be the most dangerous. A rose has thorns, a sunset can blind you if you stare too long, and a song can lure sailors to their death on the rocks."

She dismounted and knelt by the stream, cupping the clear water in her hands to drink. The liquid was cold and sweet, with a faint taste of minerals and growing things. As she drank, she caught sight of her reflection in the water – her face was cleaner than it should have been after sleeping on the forest floor, and her hair was free of the tangles and debris she would have expected.

"Henry, look at yourself," she said, gesturing toward the stream. "We should be filthy after sleeping rough, but we look as if we've just bathed."

Henry peered at his own reflection and saw that she was right. His face was clean, his hair neat, and even his tunic seemed to have been brushed free of dirt and leaves. "The trees," he said with wonder. "They must have cared for us while we slept."

"Or cast some spell upon us," Kira corrected, though her voice held less suspicion than before. Perhaps the ancient guardians of the forest were not enemies after all, but protectors of those who sought to help rather than harm.

They remounted and continued westward, the sun climbing higher overhead as they rode. The trail began to slope downward, and soon they could hear the sound of moving water ahead – not the gentle babble of a stream, but the deeper, more substantial sound of a river in motion.

♠

The trees thinned as they approached what Henry first thought was a wide river cutting through the landscape from north to south. The water stretched before them, perhaps two hundred yards across, with what appeared to be the opposite shore visible in the distance. Beyond the far bank, the land looked different – less forested, more open, with rolling hills that caught the sunlight.

"We'll have to cross here if we want to reach Owen's location," Kira said, studying the water with a tactical eye. "The trees are too thick on this side to ride north along the bank."

Henry dismounted and pulled out a brass astrolabe that Nesta had given him, along with her distance-measuring technique. He held out his thumb at arm's length, closing one eye and then the other as she had taught him.

"The mountains to the north," he said, pointing toward distant peaks barely visible on the horizon. "Using Nesta's method, I'd estimate we're about sixteen furlongs from where the Romalanders were probably harvesting trees. If we can cross here and head north on the other side, we should reach them within a few hours."

Kira nodded approvingly. For all her mixed feelings about the beautiful mapmaker, she had to admit that Nesta's knowledge was proving useful. "The water doesn't look too deep, and the current seems manageable. Julius is a strong swimmer."

They began to unpack their gear, redistributing the weight to make swimming easier for the horses. Henry filled their water skins and wrapped their food in oiled cloth to keep it dry during the crossing. As he worked, he couldn't help but think of their morning's strange awakening.

"Kira," he said carefully, "do you think the trees were telling us the truth? About the Romalanders taking their children?"

She paused in her preparations, considering the question. "I saw the vision they showed us. Owen and his men cutting down saplings, loading them into their cart like they were nothing more than firewood. The pain in Francis's voice when she spoke of her children..." Kira shook her head. "Yes, I believe them. The question is whether we can find Owen's group and convince them to return what they've stolen."

"And if they refuse?"

Kira's hand moved unconsciously to her sword hilt. "Then we make them understand that some things are worth fighting for."

Henry studied her profile as she stared across the water, noting the determined set of her jaw and the fierce light in her eyes. This was the Kira he knew best – the warrior princess who would face any danger to protect those who couldn't protect themselves. Even if those in need of protection were enchanted trees in a forest most people considered mythical.

"You've changed," he said quietly.

She turned to look at him, one eyebrow raised in question. "How so?"

"A few days ago, you would have dismissed the talking trees as unimportant. You would have assumed the saplings were just wood, nothing more. But now..." He gestured toward the forest behind them. "Now you're ready to risk your life to save the children of trees you've known for less than a day."

Kira was quiet for a long moment, her gaze distant. "Perhaps the trees changed me. Or perhaps I'm finally learning what my mother tried to teach me – that a wise ruler protects all her subjects, even the ones others don't believe exist."

She mounted Julius and urged him toward the water's edge. "Come on. The day is getting warm, and the crossing will be easier before the afternoon heat makes the horses sluggish."

♠

The water was indeed deeper than it had appeared from shore. By the time they reached the middle of the supposed river, both horses were swimming strongly, their heads held high as their riders encouraged them forward. The current was more

89

powerful than expected, pushing them steadily southward even as they struggled to maintain their westward course.

Henry found himself thinking of Nesta again as he fought to keep Augusta moving in the right direction. The mapmaker had taught him to read the land, to understand the relationship between water and terrain, to recognize the signs that indicated what lay ahead. But something about this crossing felt wrong.

He soon realized the problem; the water was too vast, too deep. Rivers in this part of the country were typically shallow and easily forded, fed by mountain streams and seasonal runoff. This body of water had the feel of something much larger, much more permanent.

As they approached what should have been the western shore, Henry realized with growing alarm that they were not reaching solid ground but rather a small island or sandbar barely large enough for the horses to stand. The water continued beyond in all directions, stretching to the horizon with no sign of an opposite bank.

"Kira!" he called out as they dragged themselves and their mounts onto the narrow strip of sand and marsh grass. "This isn't a river at all!"

She turned to look at him, water streaming from her hair and clothes, and saw the concern in his eyes. Following his gaze, she studied the water that surrounded their tiny refuge on all sides. The realization hit her like a physical blow.

"The sea," she breathed. "We're not crossing a river – we're standing on a sandbar in the middle of the sea."

Henry nodded grimly, pulling out his water skin and taking a tentative sip of the liquid inside. The taste confirmed his fears – salt and brine, unmistakably oceanic. "That's why the water was so salty when we filled our skins this morning. We thought it was just minerals from the rocks, but..."

"But it was seawater all along," Kira finished. She kicked at a piece of driftwood that had washed up on their small refuge. "This changes everything. If we're surrounded by the sea, then Owen and his men could be anywhere. They might not even be in these lands at all."

The implications of their mistake settled over them like a cold fog. They had been so focused on following the trail westward, so confident in their ability to track their enemies, that they had failed to recognize the most basic geographical reality of their situation. For the first time, Kira regretted leaving Nesta behind.

As if he was reading her thoughts, Henry sat down heavily on a piece of weathered wood, his head in his hands. "Nesta's maps," he said quietly. "She would have known. If we had brought her with us, she would have recognized the signs, warned us before we got ourselves stranded out here."

Kira felt a familiar stab of irritation at Henry's mention of the beautiful mapmaker, but this time it was tempered by the uncomfortable recognition that Henry was right. Her pride and jealousy had led them astray, and now they were trapped on a sandbar with no clear way forward.

"You're right about Nesta," she admitted reluctantly. "I should have listened to her grandfather's notes, should have paid more attention to her knowledge of the western territories. Instead, I let my... my feelings cloud my judgment."

Henry looked up at her, surprise evident on his face. It was rare for Kira to admit any kind of mistake, and even rarer for her to acknowledge that someone else might have been better equipped for a task she had undertaken.

"What feelings?" he asked gently.

Kira turned away, ostensibly to study the water around them but really to hide the flush that crept up her neck. "Nothing important. Just... I don't trust her motives."

"Because she's half Romalander?"

"Because she makes you smile in ways I've never seen before," Kira said before she could stop herself. The words hung in the salt air between them, and she immediately regretted letting them escape.

Henry was quiet for a long moment, processing what she had said. When he finally spoke, his voice was soft and uncertain. "Kira, I didn't know... I mean, I never thought..."

"Don't," she said sharply, cutting him off. "Don't say anything. It was foolish of me to... to feel anything about your friendship with her. You have every right to befriend whomever you choose."

"But I want to understand," Henry persisted. "If you thought I was interested in Nesta, why didn't you say something sooner? Why let it affect the quest?"

Kira finally turned to face him, her eyes bright with unshed tears and something that might have been anger or might have been pain. "Because I'm supposed to be the ruler of Latavia someday, Henry. I'm supposed to be focused on the good of the kingdom, not on... not on whether my best friend finds another girl more interesting than me."

The honesty of her admission seemed to surprise them both. They stood facing each other on the small sandbar, the vast sea around them and the weight of unspoken feelings between them.

"More interesting than you?" Henry said with a soft laugh. "Kira, no one could be more interesting than you. Nesta is beautiful and intelligent, yes, but she's never made me feel the way..."

He stopped himself, shaking his head. "This isn't the time or place for this conversation."

"Then when?" Kira asked, her voice barely above a whisper. "When we get back to the castle? When you're assigned to some distant posting? When my father arranges a marriage for me with some foreign prince?"

Henry stepped closer, close enough that she could see the water droplets still clinging to his eyelashes. "I don't know when," he said honestly. "But I know that whatever happens, whatever duties we're called to fulfill, you'll always be the most important person in my life."

Kira felt her breath catch in her throat. "Even though I'm difficult? Even though I'm jealous and stubborn and quick to anger?"

"Especially because of those things," Henry said with a smile. "You wouldn't be Kira without them." He leaned a little closer, and then he heard a humming noise. It wasn't coming from Kira.

Looking up, they saw a swarm of the giant fireflies approaching from the east, their wings catching the afternoon sunlight as they flew in formation toward the west.

"The fireflies from Nesta's grandfather's notes," Kira said, shading her eyes to get a better look at the creatures. "They're heading in the same direction we were trying to go."

Henry watched the swarm pass overhead, noting their purposeful flight pattern. "Maybe they know something we don't. If they're traveling west, there might be land in that direction after all."

As the fireflies disappeared into the distance, Kira's eyes brightened. "We'll find a way off this sandbar," Kira said with renewed determination. "And we'll complete our mission to save the saplings. But first, we need to figure out exactly where we are and how to get where we need to go."

Henry nodded, pulling out Nesta's extra brass compass and astrolabe. He had put it in his packs to learn how to use them later and for safekeeping. He felt a stab of regret when he realized that he had considered giving up the knighthood and becoming a mapmaker. "Let's put Nesta's tools to good use, shall we?"

Kira smiled – the first genuine smile she had given at the mention of Nesta's name. "Fine. If we're going to save the day, we might as well do it properly."

Chapter 9 - Giant Fireflies

The morning mist had long since burned away under the climbing sun, but there was still no sign of Princess Kira and Henry returning to the mapmaking camp.

Nesta sat cross-legged on a fallen log, her leather-bound notebook open but forgotten in her lap as she stared toward the western forest where her two companions had disappeared the previous day.

Mark and James returned to camp empty-handed for the third time that morning, their faces flushed with exertion and their clothes torn from pushing through thick underbrush. They had been searching since dawn, following various trails that all seemed to lead nowhere.

"Nothing," Mark announced, collapsing heavily beside the dying campfire. "We followed their horse tracks for about two miles, but then the trail just... disappears."

"Like they vanished into thin air," James added, reaching for one of the water skins and drinking deeply. "Which is impossible, unless..."

He trailed off, but everyone knew what he was thinking. The enchanted forest was legendary for making travelers disappear without a trace. But was that a story or the truth?

Peek and Aboo sat nearby under the shade of a massive oak tree, their usual cheerful demeanor replaced by obvious worry. Freddy the frog perched on a rock between them, his bulging eyes darting nervously from person to person.

"Maybe the screaming frogs ate them," Aboo said quietly, his voice carrying genuine distress.

"Frogs don't eat people," Peek corrected, but his tone suggested he wasn't entirely certain. "Do they, Freddy?"

The talking frog puffed out his throat sac indignantly. "We most certainly do not eat humans! We're quite civilized, thank you very much. Though I can't speak for all the creatures in this forest..."

Nesta closed her notebook with a sharp snap that made everyone turn toward her. "How long have you known Henry and the princess?" she asked the twins directly.

"Since they saved us from the monstrous mountain," Peek replied. "That was during their first quest together."

"And in all that time, have they ever been gone for a full night without sending word back to their companions?"

Aboo shook his massive head. "Never. Henry always comes back to check on us. Even when we're playing hide-and-seek, he never stays hidden past supper time."

"Princess Kira might be stubborn and difficult," Peek added, "but she's responsible. She wouldn't abandon her troop without good reason."

Mark laughed harshly, the sound carrying no humor. "Responsible? The same princess who stormed out of her own birthday party because people laughed at her quest? The same girl who probably dragged poor Henry off on some wild adventure just to prove she's braver than everyone thinks?"

"And Henry's just as bad," James chimed in, his voice taking on a mocking tone. "Following her around like a lovesick puppy, ready to charge into danger just because Princess Kira thinks it's a good idea."

"They're probably off somewhere playing at being heroes," Mark continued, warming to his theme. "Fighting imaginary enemies or trying to befriend some other talking animals. They'll come crawling back when they get hungry enough."

Nesta felt her temper flare at their casual dismissal of genuine concern. These men were supposed to be knights, sworn to protect their princess, yet they showed more interest in mocking her than finding her.

"That's enough," she said, rising to her feet with the fluid grace that seemed to characterize all her movements. "Whether you respect them or not, Princess Kira and Sir Henry are missing. As the only person here with actual tracking and navigation skills, I'm taking charge of this search."

Mark's eyebrows shot up in surprise. "Taking charge? You're a mapmaker, not a military commander."

"I'm the granddaughter of George the Geographer," Nesta replied coolly. "I've spent my entire life learning to read landscapes, track movements, and navigate unknown territories. More importantly, I'm the only one here who seems to actually care about finding our missing companions."

She began gathering her mapping equipment with efficient movements, checking her compass and astrolabe before securing them in her saddlebags. Nesta was thankful that she gave Henry her extra one and a few brief lessons on how to use them. With the proper tools, you're never lost. "From now on, we do this properly. No more random wandering through the forest hoping to stumble across their trail. We'll use systematic search patterns, document what we find, and make logical decisions based on evidence rather than assumptions."

James stood up, his face flushing with anger. "You can't just decide to take command of a royal military expedition. We're knights of Latavia, and you're..." He gestured vaguely, searching for words that wouldn't be openly insulting.

"I'm what?" Nesta asked dangerously, her voice taking on the same cold authority that Princess Kira used when her patience was exhausted. "Half Romalander? A woman? Someone without noble blood?"

"You're not qualified to lead knights into potentially dangerous situations," Mark said, trying to sound reasonable despite the obvious tension in his voice.

Freddy hopped closer to the argument, his eyes bright with interest. In the wild, conflicts over pack leadership were common, and he recognized the signs of a dominance struggle brewing. "Actually," the frog interjected, "from what I've observed, she's the most qualified person here. She knows the terrain, understands navigation, and has been making intelligent observations while the rest of you have been stumbling around blindly."

"Nobody asked you, frog," James snapped.

"His name is Freddy," Aboo said quietly, but with surprising firmness. "And he's been helpful. More helpful than some people."

The implied criticism hit its mark. Mark's face darkened as he realized that even the trolls were questioning his competence. "Fine," he said, his voice tight with wounded pride. "Let the mapmaker play at being a commander. But when this goes wrong, don't expect us to take responsibility for the consequences."

"I wouldn't dream of it," Nesta replied smoothly. "In fact, I think it would be best if you two remain here at the base camp while the rest of us conduct the actual search."

"Absolutely not," James protested. "We're not staying behind while civilians wander off into the enchanted forest."

"Then you'll follow my orders without question," Nesta said, her tone brooking no argument. "No more unauthorized searches, no more dismissive comments about our missing companions, and no more undermining my authority in front of the others."

She turned to address Peek and Aboo directly. "Are you willing to help me find Henry and Princess Kira?"

The twins exchanged a look and nodded in unison. "Henry is our friend," Peek said simply. "We'll do whatever it takes to find him."

"Good. Freddy, I assume you're willing to assist as well?"

The frog puffed himself up proudly. "My nose never lies, and my knowledge of this forest is extensive. Of course I'll help."

Nesta shouldered her pack and walked over to her horse, a graceful mare that had been bred for endurance rather than speed. "We'll start by retracing their last known path, but this time we'll look for signs that the rest of you missed. Broken branches at unusual heights, disturbed ground that doesn't match normal horse traffic, anything that suggests they encountered something out of the ordinary."

As she prepared to mount, Mark made one last attempt to assert his authority. "This is mutiny," he declared. "When we return to the castle, I'll be reporting your insubordination to King Phillip himself."

Nesta paused with one foot in the stirrup and looked back at him with an expression of mild amusement. "By all means, report that the half-Romalander mapmaker took charge when the Latavian knights proved more interested in mockery than in actually finding their missing princess. I'm sure His Majesty will be fascinated to hear how you handled the situation."

With that, she swung gracefully into her saddle and looked down at the assembled group. "Anyone who wants to help find our friends can follow me. Anyone who prefers to sit around making jokes can stay here and explain to Princess Kira why you didn't bother looking for her when she fails to return."

Peek and Aboo immediately began the complex process of coordinating their movement toward their shared horse, a massive draft animal that was the only mount strong enough to carry their combined weight. Freddy hopped onto Peek's shoulder with obvious satisfaction.

"This should be interesting," the frog commented quietly. "I haven't seen this much drama since the great territorial dispute between the eastern and western frog clans."

Mark and James watched in frustration as their authority crumbled. They could refuse to follow Nesta's lead, but that would mean staying behind while others searched for the princess. Their pride warred with their duty, and duty ultimately won.

"This isn't over," Mark muttered as he mounted his own horse.

"No," Nesta agreed, adjusting her reins with practiced ease. "It's just beginning. Now let's go find our friends before something terrible happens to them."

♠

The swarm of Giant Fireflies moved with purpose and intelligence, their flight pattern coordinated like a military formation. As they drew closer, both Kira and Henry could see that these were no ordinary insects – their eyes glowed with predatory intelligence, and their mandibles clicked with anticipation.

"We need to find shelter," Kira said, but even as she spoke, the swarm adjusted its course directly toward them.

The giant fireflies descended upon them like a living storm cloud. There were dozens of them, each one easily the size of a hawk, with wings that hummed with supernatural speed and bodies that glowed with an eerie phosphorescence even in the bright afternoon sunlight.

Henry's first instinct was to draw his sword, but the creatures moved too quickly, darting and weaving through the air with impossible agility. One landed on his arm and immediately sank its mandibles into his flesh, drawing blood and eliciting a cry of pain and surprise.

"They're biting!" he shouted, swatting at the creature only to have two more take its place.

Kira drew her sword and began swinging it through the air in elaborate patterns, trying to drive off the attackers, but the fireflies seemed to anticipate her movements, dodging her blade with mocking ease. Several landed on her shoulders and arms, their bites feeling like hot needles driven into her skin.

"Run!" she commanded, wheeling Julius around and spurring him toward the forest edge. "We need cover!"

They galloped toward a stand of thick trees, the swarm pursuing them with relentless determination. Every few yards, more fireflies would dive down to attack, leaving bloody wounds on their arms and necks. The creatures seemed particularly drawn to exposed skin, and both riders found themselves hunching over their horses' necks to present smaller targets.

As they reached the tree line, Henry suddenly pulled up short. "Wait!" he called out, an idea forming in his mind. "Nesta's notes said they were fierce, but she didn't say they were evil. What if they're just protecting their territory?"

Kira turned back, her face flushed with anger and streaked with small puncture wounds. "Protecting it from what? Us?"

"Maybe," Henry said, watching as the swarm hovered at the edge of the meadow, as if reluctant to follow them into the deeper forest. "Or maybe they're responding to something else entirely."

Henry studied the creatures more carefully, noting how they moved in coordinated patterns and seemed to communicate through rapid flashes of light. "What if we could use them?" he asked quietly.

"Use them how?"

Instead of answering directly, Henry reached into his saddlebag and pulled out a piece of dried meat from their provisions. He held it up experimentally, and immediately several of the fireflies oriented toward him, their antennae twitching with interest.

"They're hungry," he said with growing excitement. "And if they're hungry enough..."

Without waiting for Kira's response, Henry tossed the meat into the air. The nearest firefly caught it with remarkable dexterity, immediately attracting the attention of its companions. Within moments, the entire swarm was focused on the food rather than the humans.

"Brilliant," Kira breathed, understanding his plan immediately. She reached into her own pack and pulled out more provisions. "But we'll need something bigger than dried meat if we want to control a whole swarm."

Henry grinned, reaching deeper into Augusta's saddlebags. "Remember when you said we packed too much food? I think you're about to change your mind."

♠

As the green troop moved to the west, Freddy rode on the troll's shoulder.

"Tell us more about these giant fireflies," Aboo said, "Are they really as fierce as the stories say?"

103

Freddy's throat sac pulsed with nervous energy. "Oh, they're fierce all right," he croaked. "About the size of a bird, like I told you before. But it's not their size that makes them dangerous – it's their appetite."

"What do they eat?" Peek asked, glancing worriedly at the pot where several of Freddy's relatives floated in various stages of preparation.

"Whatever they want," Freddy replied grimly. "They especially like frogs, but they'll take birds, small mammals, even insects larger than themselves. When they hunt in a swarm, they can bring down prey many times their size."

Mark looked rode up closer, he had been listening. "How do you kill something like that?"

"You don't," Freddy said bluntly. "When you see a swarm coming, you have three choices: hide, run, or pray. Preferably all three."

James laughed harshly. "What about fighting them? They're just insects."

Freddy fixed him with a look that was remarkably expressive for an amphibian. "Have you ever tried to swat a regular firefly? Now imagine it's the size of your fist, moves twice as fast, and has mandibles that can pierce leather. And there are fifty of them."

"So how do the other animals survive?" Nesta asked, looking up from her sketching with genuine curiosity.

"Various ways," Freddy explained, warming to his subject. "Some dig burrows and hide underground. Others have learned to recognize the warning signs and clear out before the swarms arrive. And a few..." He paused dramatically. "A few have learned to negotiate."

"Negotiate with insects?" Mark scoffed.

"They're not just insects," Freddy corrected. "They're intelligent. They can learn, adapt, even problem-solve. And they have excellent memories for both friends and enemies."

Aboo nudged Peek with his elbow. "Maybe that's why Kira and Henry haven't come back yet. Maybe they ran into a swarm."

"Don't say that," Peek replied nervously. "Henry promised he'd come back to play with us."

Nesta looked toward the western forest with concern. The afternoon was wearing on, and there had been no sign of the princess and Henry.

Freddy's eyes swiveled between the speakers, and he made a decision. "If you're really worried about your friends," he said to Nesta, "I could try to track them. We frogs have an excellent sense of smell."

"You'd do that?" Peek asked hopefully.

"For Henry, yes," Freddy replied. "He's one of the few humans who bothered to listen before trying to eat me."

♠

Meanwhile, back at Owen's increasingly desperate camp, the three Romalanders were discovering just how difficult it had become to harvest the enchanted saplings. What had started as a simple wood-gathering expedition had turned into something approaching warfare.

Owen wiped sweat from his brow as he struggled with a particularly stubborn sapling. Every time he managed to cut through one root, two more seemed to sprout in its place. The tree fought back with an intelligence that was both remarkable and deeply unsettling.

"These roots are getting thicker," Bart complained, wrestling with his shovel as it became tangled in a network of woody tendrils. "And I swear they're moving on their own."

Dirk paused in his digging to examine his tools. His axe blade was noticeably duller than when they'd started, and his shovel showed signs of unusual wear. "It's like they're fighting back," he said uneasily.

Owen stepped back from his work and surveyed their progress with growing frustration. They had been laboring since dawn, but their cart was only half full. At this rate, it would take them days to gather enough timber to satisfy Prince William's demands.

"We need to try a different approach," he decided. "Instead of fighting these trees individually, let's see if we can dig up an entire section at once."

He directed his companions to begin excavating around a cluster of young saplings, hoping that by working together they could overcome the trees' mysterious resistance. But as soon as they began their coordinated effort, the forest around them erupted into activity.

Roots burst from the ground like serpents, wrapping around their tools and trying to wrench them away. Branches swayed without any wind, and leaves rustled with what sounded disturbingly like whispered conversations. The very air seemed to thicken with opposition to their efforts.

"Maybe we should reconsider this whole mission," Bart suggested nervously, jumping back as a particularly aggressive root made a grab for his ankle.

"Prince William is paying us too well to give up now," Owen replied grimly. "These trees may be magical, but they're still just trees. We'll find a way."

♠

Back in the meadow where the giant fireflies had first attacked, Kira and Henry had managed to attract a substantial portion of the swarm using their food supplies as bait. The creatures hovered around them in a loose cloud, their wings humming with barely contained energy as they waited for more offerings.

"Now what?" Kira asked, eyeing the swarm nervously. "We've got their attention, but how do we direct it where we want it to go?"

Henry studied the fireflies' behavior, noting how they responded to movement and sound. "Watch this," he said, tossing another piece of meat. Several fireflies immediately darted after it, only to return when they realized it was too far to safely retrieve.

"We'd need more than what we're carrying," Kira pointed out practically. "And even if we had enough food, what's to stop them from eating it all and then turning on us again?"

Henry grinned, reaching into Augusta's saddlebags one more time. "Remember those extra rope and supplies you complained about? I think it's time you appreciated my overpacking."

He pulled out a coil of rope and began fashioning a crude net. "If we can catch a few of them without hurting them, we might be able to use them as... guides."

Kira watched with growing admiration as Henry worked. His plan was audacious and potentially dangerous, but it showed the kind of creative thinking that had made him invaluable during their previous adventures.

"You want to use giant fireflies as flying mounts," she said slowly. "That's either brilliant or completely insane."

"Probably both," Henry admitted. "But it's better than trying to fight our way through a swarm of them to reach the Romalander's camp on foot. Unless, you'd like to fly?"

Kira grew angry. "I will never fly again, you know that!"

"Then let's hope this works." As if to prove his point, a distant buzzing reached their ears – another swarm approaching from the direction of the Romalander camp. The fireflies around them grew agitated, their lights pulsing in what seemed like a communication pattern.

"Looks like they're coordinating," Kira observed. "Whatever Owen's been doing, he's managed to anger more than just the trees."

Henry finished his improvised net and looked at Kira seriously. "Are you ready to try something that's never been attempted before?"

Kira drew her sword and tested its balance, then looked at the swarm of giant fireflies surrounding them. Her raptor blood stirred with longing for the skies, but she pushed down the urge to spread her wings. Instead, she focused on the task at hand.

"Let's catch ourselves some fireflies," she said with grim determination. Soon, the nets were filled and they were lifted into the sky toward the Romalander camp.

Chapter 10 - The Hidden Road

The fireflies flew Henry and Kira closer and closer to the Romanlander camp. Below them, their horses galloped at a fast pace to keep up. Surprisingly, the horses swam across the water between the sandbar and the mainland. When they were close to smoke coming from the camp, the fireflies abruptly worked their way out of the nets, dropping Kira and Henry to the ground.

"At least we still have the horses," Henry said, pointing toward a nearby clearing where Julius and Augusta grazed peacefully on sweet grass. The animals showed no signs of distress or enchantment, which provided some small comfort.

They mounted quickly and reached a small clearing where the remains of Owen's camp lay scattered. The cart that had held the stolen saplings sat empty, its wooden sides stained with dirt from the uprooted trees. Tools lay abandoned – shovels, axes, and ropes that told the story of hasty departure.

"They're gone," Henry observed, dismounting to examine the abandoned campsite. "But look at this." He pointed to deep gouges in the earth where the saplings had been torn from their roots, and to strange burn marks on several nearby trees.

Kira knelt beside the cart and found several young saplings still lying in its bed, their roots wrapped in damp cloth. "Some of them might still be alive," she said, her voice filled with hope. "If we can get them back into the ground quickly enough, they might survive."

Working together, they carefully lifted the surviving saplings from the cart. There were seven in total – young oaks and maples, their leaves wilted but still showing signs of life. Henry began digging holes near the edge of the clearing while Kira prepared the roots for replanting.

"The trees said we had until sunset to return their children," she reminded him as they worked. "We may have lost time sleeping, but we can still save these."

As they planted the last sapling, a familiar rustling filled the air around them. The branches overhead began to sway without any wind, and the very earth seemed to pulse with life. Suddenly, thick vines descended from the canopy, but instead of binding them, the vines gently watered the newly planted saplings with drops of morning dew.

"Thank you," whispered a voice that seemed to come from all around them. It was Ida, the gentlest of the tree mothers, her ancient wisdom carried on the wind. "You have saved our children, young warriors. The forest will not forget this kindness."

More voices joined hers – Francis and Mabel, and dozens of other trees throughout the forest, all humming in harmonious gratitude. The sound was unlike anything Kira or Henry had ever heard, a song of earth and growing things that seemed to heal something deep within their souls.

"There is more you must know," Ida's voice continued, growing more serious. "The men who stole our children spoke of a hidden road – a secret path that leads from Romaland directly into our forest. This road poses a great danger to both our realm and yours."

Kira felt her blood run cold. A hidden road from Romaland could allow enemy forces to bypass Latavia's border defenses entirely, striking at the heart of the kingdom from an unexpected direction.

"Where is this road?" she asked aloud.

The wind picked up, rustling through the leaves in a pattern that seemed almost like language. Henry, who had always been good with directions, pointed toward the northwest.

"That way," he said with certainty. "The trees are showing us the path."

♠

Following the directions whispered by the forest, Kira and Henry rode for another hour before they found what they were looking for. Hidden beneath carefully arranged branches and concealed by what appeared to be natural undergrowth was a well-maintained road. The path was wide enough for carts and horses, and showed clear signs of recent use.

"This is no game trail," Kira observed grimly, dismounting to examine the wheel ruts in the dirt. "This road was built for military purposes."

Henry studied the construction with growing alarm. The road showed evidence of careful roadmaking– proper drainage, reinforced bridges over streams, and sight lines that had been deliberately cleared to allow rapid movement of troops.

"Look at this," he called, pointing to a series of carved markers along the roadside. The symbols were unmistakably Romalander – distance markers and direction signs that would allow enemy forces to navigate even in darkness.

They followed the road for several miles, documenting its path and noting key strategic points. The forest grew gradually thinner as they traveled, until finally they emerged onto a hill that overlooked the border between Latavia and Romaland. From this vantage point, they could see Romalander settlements in the distance, and more importantly, they could see that the hidden road connected directly to Romaland's main road system.

"This changes everything," Kira said, her strategic mind already calculating the implications. "Prince William or any other Romalander leader could move an entire army through this forest without our border guards ever knowing they were coming."

Henry nodded gravely. "They could strike at the capital itself before our forces could mobilize to defend it."

As they turned to head back, they heard the sound of approaching hoofbeats. Quickly concealing themselves behind a stand of trees, they watched as a group of riders emerged from the forest. To their surprise, the riders weren't Romalanders – they were their own companions.

Nesta led the group, her mapping equipment visible in her saddlebags. Behind her rode Mark and James, still wearing the green tunics of Henry's colors but looking decidedly worse for wear. Peek and Aboo brought up the rear, their massive forms making the horses look like ponies by comparison.

"Kira! Henry!" Nesta called out as she spotted them. "We've been following your trail for hours. When you didn't return to camp, we grew worried."

Freddy the frog, riding on Peek's shoulder, hopped excitedly. "I told them my nose never lies! I could smell your path even through all this enchanted forest nonsense."

"You found a road," Mark observed, his tone suggesting he understood the significance of their discovery.

"More than that," Kira replied grimly. "We found proof that Romaland has been preparing for war. This road could bring an army right to our doorstep."

Nesta dismounted and began pulling out her mapping materials. "I need to document this thoroughly," she said. "The exact route, the construction methods, the strategic implications..."

"No," Kira said firmly, her hand moving to her sword hilt. "There will be no map of this road."

Nesta looked up in surprise. "But Princess, this is exactly the kind of intelligence your father needs. A detailed map could help him plan defensive measures..."

"A detailed map could also fall into the wrong hands," Kira interrupted. "Maps can be stolen, copied, sold to enemies. The only way to ensure this road never threatens Latavia is to make sure it can't be used."

Henry studied Kira's expression and recognized the determined look that meant she had already formulated a plan. "What are you thinking?"

Kira turned to Peek and Aboo, who had been listening with growing interest. "My large friends, how good are you at moving rocks?"

The twins exchanged excited glances. "We love throwing rocks!" Peek exclaimed.

"How about moving really big rocks?" Kira pressed. "Boulder-sized rocks?"

"Even better!" Aboo added enthusiastically.

Kira smiled, the expression transforming her face from grim determination to fierce joy. "Then I have a job for you."

♠

The plan was ambitious but simple. Working together, they would systematically destroy the hidden road's usability. Peek and Aboo would handle the heavy work – rolling massive boulders from the surrounding hills to block key choke points along the route. Henry and the others would fell trees across the path and destroy the stone bridges that spanned various streams.

But the most important part of the plan involved the enchanted forest itself. Following Ida's whispered instructions, Kira led the group to several clearings along the roadway where the tree mothers had agreed to help. Using a combination of magical growth and natural processes, the trees would send roots and branches across the road, making it impassable within a matter of months.

"The forest reclaims what was taken from it," Ida's voice whispered through the leaves as they worked. "This road was carved through our heart without permission. Now our heart will heal, and the scar will disappear."

As they worked, Nesta observed the process with growing fascination. "The precision of the growth patterns is remarkable," she murmured, making notes in her journal. "If I could map the magical properties of this forest..."

"Some things shouldn't be mapped," Kira said firmly. "Some secrets are meant to stay secret."

By evening, their work was nearly complete. The main route was blocked in at least a dozen places, with more obstructions growing naturally as the forest's magic took hold.

Anyone attempting to use the road now would find it completely impassable.

As they made camp near the forest's edge, Freddy hopped over to sit beside the fire. "You know," he said thoughtfully, "I heard those Romalander soldiers talking when they first came through and were trying to eat me. They mentioned something about Prince William having bigger plans for next year."

"What kind of plans?" Henry asked, leaning forward with interest.

"Something about a grand invasion once the harvest was complete. They kept talking about how this road was just the beginning – that there were other routes being prepared, other ways to attack Latavia when you least expected it."

Kira and Henry exchanged concerned glances. If Freddy was right, the hidden road was just one part of a larger strategy. Even with this particular threat neutralized, Romaland was clearly planning something much more ambitious.

"We need to get this information back to my father," Kira decided. "And we need to start thinking about what other surprises Prince William might have in store for us."

♠

The next morning brought an unexpected visitor. As they prepared to break camp and begin the journey home, Charles emerged from the forest with a small group of knights. His weathered face showed relief when he spotted Kira and Henry among their companions.

"Princess," he said, dismounting and offering a respectful bow. "Your father sends word that you and Sir Henry are to return to the capital immediately. There have been developments."

"What kind of developments?" Kira asked, her stomach tightening with worry.

"Prince William has sent ambassadors to the court," Charles explained. "They claim to come in peace, seeking to negotiate a new treaty between our kingdoms. But intelligence suggests they may actually be advance scouts, gathering information for a future attack."

Kira nodded grimly. After discovering the hidden road, the news didn't surprise her. "We have information that will be valuable to those negotiations," she said. "Prince William has been planning more than diplomatic missions."

She quickly explained their discovery of the road and the evidence they had found of Romalander military preparations. Charles listened with growing concern, occasionally asking pointed questions about specific details.

"This explains much," he said when she finished. "Your father suspected something when the ambassadors arrived with unusually detailed knowledge of our border defenses. If they've been scouting through this forest..."

"Not anymore," Henry interjected with satisfaction. "That road is now completely unusable."

Charles smiled approvingly. "Well done, both of you. But this raises new questions about Prince William's ultimate intentions."

As they prepared to depart, Peek and Aboo approached Kira with slightly downcast expressions.

"Do we have to go back to our cave now? Romalanders kill trolls." Peek asked sadly.

"We liked having friends," Aboo added. "It made us feel... useful."

"The choice is yours," she said finally. "You can return to your cave if that's what makes you happy. Or..."

"Or?" both twins asked eagerly.

"Or you can stay a part of Henry's green troop. I'm sure Sir Henry could find work for two strong, loyal friends of the crown. Plus, the castle always needs help with construction projects, and there's a nice stable where you could live, now that Sir Henry will live in the knights' quarters."

The twins exchanged delighted glances. "We choose Henry!" they exclaimed in unison.

Henry added, "I'd like to keep Freddy too."

Freddy hopped onto Peek's shoulder with a satisfied croak. "Good choice. I've always wanted to see a real castle."

♠

The journey back to Latavia took three days, with the expanded group making slower progress than Kira and Henry would have alone. Nesta rode beside Henry for much of the journey, and Kira found herself watching their interactions with curiosity rather than jealousy.

The beautiful mapmaker clearly admired Henry's quick thinking and brave actions, while Henry seemed genuinely interested in her knowledge of geography and navigation. As if he felt it, Henry gave Augusta a little kick and caught up with Kira.

Kira was deep in thought about Prince William who seemed to want to play diplomatic games while planning for war. She turned to Henry as he joined her.

"Two can play this game. I'll ask my father to send us to Prince William's court as representatives of Latavia, ostensibly to finalize the details of whatever treaty his ambassadors negotiate now. But my real mission will be to gather intelligence about his true intentions and capabilities."

Henry leaned toward her with excitement. "A reconnaissance mission disguised as a diplomatic visit to Romanland?"

"Precisely. Prince William will expect us to send experienced diplomats – older, more predictable men who will follow traditional protocols. He won't expect us to send Latavia's heir and a young knight."

Kira felt a thrill of excitement at the prospect. After spending so much time learning about warfare and statecraft, the opportunity to engage in real diplomatic intrigue was appealing.

"When do we leave?" he asked.

"Most likely, in one month's time. That will give Prince William's ambassadors time to return home and report on their visit here. It will also give you time to prepare for what will be a very different kind of quest."

As they continued their journey home, Kira asked, "Are you ready for this? Diplomatic missions can be just as dangerous as military ones, but in different ways."

Henry smiled, feeling more confident than he ever had. "With you beside me? I'm ready for anything." Henry wasn't sure he should tell her that he had another mission-to find his roots.

Like those saplings, he had been pulled away from his home. "Besides," Henry added with a grin, "how dangerous could a simple diplomatic mission to Romaland possibly be?"

Kira laughed, "Hopefully less treacherous than facing talking trees, screaming frogs and giant fireflies!"

THE END

Coming Soon: "Dangerous Treaty" - Princess Kira and Sir Henry travel to Prince William's court in Romaland to negotiate a new treaty, but the strange customs and hidden dangers of the Romalander capital prove more challenging than any enchanted forest.

The massive wooden doors of Latavia's great hall shuddered on their hinges as Peek and Aboo tumbled through them in their characteristic awkward fashion, their conjoined form making even simple entrances an adventure. They clutched several large platters of roasted meat that had been destined for the visiting Romalander delegation's welcoming feast.

"Sorry, sorry!" Aboo called out breathlessly as chunks of perfectly seasoned beef scattered across the polished stone floor.

"We were trying to help!" Peek added, his face flushed with embarrassment as he attempted to gather the fallen food while still attached to his brother.

The dozen Romalander nobles seated at the high table watched this display with expressions ranging from disgust to outright horror. At their head sat Prince William, his handsome features twisted into a mask of barely controlled revulsion as he observed the twins' clumsy efforts to clean up their mess.

"Trolls," he said, his cultured voice dripping with disdain. "In a civilized dining hall. How... progressive of you, Princess Kira."

Kira, seated across from the prince, maintained his diplomatic composure despite the tension crackling through the air. "Peek and Aboo have proven themselves loyal friends to the crown. They fought beside Henry to save the enchanted forest."

"Ah yes, the enchanted forest," Prince William mused, dabbing at his lips with a silk napkin though he had not yet touched his food. "Where creatures like these belong. Along with other... aberrations that civilized society cannot tolerate."

Princess Kira, felt her raptor blood stir dangerously at the veiled threat. Her hand moved instinctively toward her sword hilt, but a gentle touch on her arm from Henry stayed her action.

"In Romaland," Prince William continued, his cold gaze fixed on the still-struggling trolls, "we have maintained order for centuries by ensuring that monsters remain where they belong – in the wild places, far from decent people. Some bloodlines are simply too dangerous to integrate into proper society."

"Perhaps," Henry said, stepping forward with careful diplomacy, "our upcoming visit to your court will help bridge some of these... cultural differences between our peoples."

Prince William's attention shifted to Henry with predatory interest. "Ah yes, Sir Henry. The sapling from Romaland. I confess myself curious about your origins. It's so rare for one of our people to rise so high in Latavian society."

Henry's jaw tightened slightly, but his voice remained steady. "I hope to learn more about my heritage during our diplomatic mission. Perhaps there are records in Romaland that could shed light on my family's history."

"Oh, I'm certain we can arrange something," Prince William replied, his smile sharp as a snake's teeth. "Romaland keeps very detailed records of its bloodlines. Very detailed indeed. Once a Romalander..."

The Complete Kira and Henry Series:

- Book 1: Quest into the Forbidden Lands
- Book 2: Lost in the Enchanted Forest
- Book 3: Dangerous Treaty (Coming Soon)
- Book 4: War Games (Coming Soon)
- Book 5: Edict of Love (Coming Soon)
- Book 6: King Kira (Coming Soon)

About the Author

Sandi Jerome is a writer and graduate of UCLA's Advanced Screenwriting program. Her screenplay, Runaway Cricket, is being produced as an animated musical by BlackOrb.com.

Sandi is an enrolled and blood member of the Cherokee Nation and a 2023 Native American Media Alliance fellow - twice. In her first NAMA TV writing fellowship, she wrote Technically Soccer, a half-hour comedy about a Women's Professional Soccer team getting an AI-Robot coach. It is being developed into a TV series by Little Studio Films. Sandi is an avid women's soccer fan; she has coached, played, and refereed soccer for over twenty years.

Her middle-grade book, Sleep Warrior, about her Cherokee ancestor, is on Coverfly's Red List as the #3 Animated Manuscripts. Sandi's family is part of the Wolf Clan of the Cherokee tribe and she has written two screenplays with wolves. NOT werewolves - these wolves are real. Blood Moon Wolf (TV Pilot and Feature) was completed as part of her 2nd Native American fellowship about a wolf turning into the girl to be a spirit guide.

She grew up on an avocado farm in Escondido and was the "go to" kid to climb up high and pick the top fruit. She would then jump down into the thick pile of leaves and thought she could fly! She created this young adult fantasy series, Kira and Henry, where the teen princess has to hide the secret that she can fly or be banished from the kingdom. The first book, Quest into the Forbidden Lands, was a 2nd Rounder in 2023 Austin Film Festival and a 2024 Kindle Book Review finalist. Lost in the Enchanted Forest continues Princess Kira and Sir Henry's adventures as they face magical trees, giant fireflies, and political intrigue while discovering the true meaning of friendship and loyalty.

The complete Kira and Henry series will span six books, following the young heroes from their first quest through Kira's coronation as King. Book 3, Dangerous Treaty, takes them into the treacherous world of Romalander politics where diplomatic missions prove more dangerous than any enchanted forest. War Games explores the complexities of medieval warfare and competition, while Edict of Love challenges Kira to balance duty with her heart's desires. The series concludes with King Kira, where the newly crowned ruler must learn that true strength comes not from wielding power alone, but from preserving the relationships that make power worth having.

Sandi is a scientist and loves designing edible gardens and doing botany experiments. Her early fascination with science and the nearby San Onofre Nuclear Generating station inspired her to write an action script, Use of Deadly Force. Her husband was a technical writer in the nuclear industry and ensured its authenticity. Sandi aims to help emerging producers and directors get their projects to the screen.

She is a native Californian, born in Santa Ana. She belonged to a Science and Technology group and helped develop a volunteer Web on Wheels program that brought email to residents of assisted living centers. This inspired her body-switching comedy, Time for Lily, which was a First-Round Finalist in Script Magazine Open Door Contest.

As a former computer programmer, she has been granted two patents for software design and recently sold her software company. She wrote a Sci-Fi thriller script, Last Woman, which involves the multi-universe and technology gone awry. It was a semifinalist in Final Draft's Big Break contest in 2023. Sandi partnered with Heidi Stangeland for the rewrite of this script and wrote another thriller with Heidi, Python Pursuit that now has a director attached.

Sandi was the first editor of Digital Dealer and wrote computer software reviews for major publications and numerous published computer guides.

As a Floridian and a long-time Disney fan, annual passholder and certified Disney expert, Sandi wrote Pixie Dust Death set at Disney World, and then created a non-Disney version set at a theme park she invented. Wilma Wallaby Genius Girl Detective is being developed into a kid's series by a UK Production company. She is also the author of the Amazing Animals of Disney's Animal Kingdom.

Sandi wrote a book adaptation of Hijacked for producer Melissa Shevela of Helicopter Productions which is being shopped by fellow producer Autumn Bailey of AB Entertainment (On a Wing and a Prayer with Dennis Quaid.) Autumn is shopping two of Sandi's Hallmark-like Christmas scripts along with a faith-based RomCom. Melissa has optioned Sandi's book, Cases of Nevada's Gaming Commission and they are developing a procedural TV series, Last Hand. Her next book adaptation to film was Jake and Clara based on the book, Jake & Clara: Scandal, Politics, Hollywood and Murder by David R. Stokes. His previous book was optioned by Blair Underwood.

Sandi is represented by Alexia Melocchi of Little Studio Films who is producing the Five Points series; Mama Dallas and Augie. Sandi wrote the screenplay for Augie and the book, published by LSF, Mama Dallas and Augie. Sandi and Alexia are working on Alexia's next book, The Heart of Show Business where Sandi will write the section on the business of show business. For Sandi, "Writing is life!"

Learn more at www.**SandraJerome**.com or leave comments at her publisher's Contact page, www.**SmilingEagle**.com.

www.ingramcontent.com/pod-product-compliance
Lightning Source LLC
Chambersburg PA
CBHW052006220626
47052CB00004B/1113